Libby's Choice

Katharine E. Matchette

Libby's Choice

Dedicated to Dennis, my husband and printing partner whose expertise made this book and DeKa Press possible.

Thanks to Susan Fawver who crossed the *t*'s, dotted the *i's*, and added perfecting touches to the manuscript. Peggy Baker assisted with proofreading. Dennis Headrick gave valuable production support. Rick Delker designed the cover.

And thanks to all my friends at Barclay Press who introduced me to the production side of publishing, and taught me to love type as well as words.

Table of Contents

Chapter 1

Arrival

The ship *Good Providence* scraped roughly against the wharf. Libby Kendall stared intently at the watchers milling about on the dock below. Nowhere could she see a man she would wish to call her master. The men below, the strange city—even the hills of Boston rising behind the harbor—all threatened her. She could not escape them. Resolutely, Libby ignored the thought and turned to her father standing beside her.

"The New World at last, Father. What do you think?"

Jeremiah Kendall beamed. "The City of God," he said. "Our land of freedom."

"Is it?" Libby asked, eyeing the potential buyers of indentures who milled on the dock below. "We'll be the same as slaves for at least four years until we've worked off our passage money."

"Does it scare you?" Jeremiah asked.

Father must never guess her terror. But Libby could not lie. "What about you?" she asked.

"No." Jeremiah spoke confidently. He gestured toward the crowd on the dock below. "They may buy our indentures and own our service, but they are our brothers—Puritans like us."

His words encouraged Libby. "Then I won't be afraid either." She stood as tall as she could and resettled her cap carefully over her blonde hair. They had come safely this far. She could not lose heart now.

Nothing discouraged Father; not the prospect of four years of virtual slavery; not even spending the first part of their voyage confined to his pallet in the hold with seasickness. Then during their two-month layover in Barbados, he had caught dysentery and a tropical fever. If it had not been for Goodman Isaac Matthews . . . Libby smiled, remembering. Goodman Matthews had exchanged his own down comforter for Father's worn blanket when Father shook with chills. Each day Mr. Matthews had descended into the hold with food and wine. During the two worst days he had carried Father to his cabin and nursed him there. Perhaps some day in the New World Libby could return his kindness.

The steady ship and fresh air had restored a little pink to her father's cheeks, but he had regained little strength. How could he do a day's work?

The Mate came among the steerage passengers ordering all able-bodied men to help the stevedores unload cargo. Jeremiah wobbled forward. The Mate shook his head. "Save your strength."

"Thank you, so much, Sir," Libby said. Since her mother died four years ago, Libby had done her best to help and protect her father. But she could not influence her father's buying—or collect accounts as her mother had.

When the *Good Providence* had docked in London Libby saw it as their only hope. "You have to go, Father. You saw the notice from the leather company. They'll have you in debtor's prison by next week."

"We'll pay—" Father had begun. But Libby pulled out the account book.

"We have the money coming. But there's no way to collect it. They won't listen to me."

"I can't rob the poor."

Libby sighed. "We're poor. And you can't help anyone if you're in debtor's prison. I've already talked to the captain of the *Good Providence*."

"It's not what I want for you, Libby."

"I can earn my freedom there. Here they'd send us both to prison. How could we earn our way out?"

In the end Father had given in. By the time they sailed, his excitement outdid her own.

Two seamen let down the gangplank with a crash, interrupting Libby's thoughts. She and all the steerage passengers watched as half a dozen stevedores scrambled aboard, followed by several well-dressed businessmen. The waiting steerage passengers exchanged apprehensive glances. These businessmen controlled their destiny. Whose indentures would they buy?

One man headed straight toward Libby as soon as he reached the deck. Her heart pounding, she studied him closely. He dressed plainly but his clothes were whole and good, Libby saw. Like her father and his friends, the man wore the familiar "roundhead" close-cropped hairstyle of the Puritans.

He walks as though he were used to getting his way, Libby thought, trying to decide if his face looked cross, or merely sober.

For a moment fear attacked her. She felt Father's hand rest lightly on her shoulder. Without looking, she knew he stood with closed eyes, praying courage for her. When the man stopped beside her she gave him her best smile.

"Good morning, daughter. My name is Joseph Rowlandson. What might thou be called?"

"Elizabeth Kendall—Libby for short."

"And how old are you?"

"Seventeen, Sir."

"What brings you to Boston?"

"My Father, Sir." Libby moved closer to Jeremiah. "His shop in London burned in the great fire when I was a baby. After my mother died, debts grew faster than the business."

"I see." Mr. Rowlandson frowned thoughtfully, glancing from Libby to her father. "What canst thou do, Libby Kendall?"

"Almost anything." Libby flushed. She hadn't meant to boast. "I-I mean my mother died when I was thirteen. At home I did the laundry, cooking, marketing, and made most of our clothing. I also helped Father with his accounts."

Mr. Rowlandson smiled. "And what kind of accounting did you do?"

"Collecting, Sir. Father hated to ask anyone to pay what they owed. But I didn't." Libby stopped abruptly. What would Master Rowlandson think of such boasting?

"She has a good business head," Father said. He smiled ruefully, "Better than mine, I know."

Mr. Rowlandson actually laughed. "I don't have accounts to collect. I am a pastor. But my wife needs a girl to help with housework and laundry and to care for our five-year-old daughter."

"I'd love that!" Libby said, thinking of her baby brothers—all buried in London.

Pastor Rowlandson turned to Father. "With your daughter's experience I'm sure she will do nicely for us," he said. "You need have no fear for her welfare. She will be fed and clothed and we will see to her spiritual instruction."

"Thank you," Jeremiah said. "This was my one prayer throughout the voyage."

Mr. Rowlandson faced Libby again. "I shall have the articles of indenture drawn up, then I'll return for you soon after noon. We'll spend the night with friends in Boston so that we may make an early start for Lancaster on the morrow."

"Is Lancaster far?" Libby asked.

"Perhaps not as the crow flies. But by horseback it is two days. You will find our roads abominable."

"Libby is a hard worker," Jeremiah assured him. "I'm relieved to see her in such good hands. I thank you."

"Until afternoon, then." The men shook hands and Master Rowlandson turned and hurried down the gangplank. Libby and her father watched him until he turned onto a side street.

"I like him," Jeremiah said.

"I-I think I like him, too." Libby agreed. "But I wish Lancaster weren't so far from Boston. How can I go without knowing about thee?"

Behind them sailors scrambled about taking down the sails. Stevedores jockeyed barrels of molasses they had taken on in the West Indies. A woman rushed into the arms of her husband, crying joyfully. Even the constable who collected a prisoner and hustled him roughly ashore failed to hold Libby's attention. She stood watching her father, trying to memorize his face. When would she see him again?

The ranks of the steerage passengers gradually thinned during the morning, but no one came for Father. At noon he and Libby sat on the deck munching the last fragments of the dry bread they had brought. *Father will never gain strength without food*, Libby thought. *Please God, send someone for him, soon.*

As though in answer to her prayer, two men strode purposefully across the deck toward them. The older man wore a well-cut dark suit with a lace cravat. Everything about him from his gently rounded middle to his ruddy, smiling face spoke of prosperity. Libby eyed him approvingly as he spoke to Father.

"And what will happen to you, Miss?" said a voice at her side.

Libby jumped. She had watched Father and the older man too closely to notice anyone else. She looked up to see the younger of the two men. She flushed, realizing he had addressed her as "you," not the familiar "thee" reserved for servants and children or close friends. "I go to Joseph Rowlandson, a pastor in Lancaster."

"He's a good man. I know him."

Libby studied the stranger carefully. Although he looked a little older than herself, he stood no more than two inches taller than she. But his body was square and sturdy. His face matched his body— square and honest looking. She read genuine concern on his face, but when his blue eyes met hers, he smiled. She couldn't help smiling back.

"Your father is not well is he?"

"All he needs is solid ground and good food."

"I couldn't help noticing. But don't worry. I won't say anything. That's my stepfather, Zedekiah Bassett, talking to him. Once home I'll see that your father gets everything he needs. By the way, I'm John Morris."

I have a friend in the New World! Libby thought. Like a good omen, the sun blazed through a wispy cloud. "I'm Libby Kendall," she said.

"I'm sure my stepfather likes your father."

Libby felt her heart pounding. "I hope so."

"I often visit the Praying Villages with Daniel Gookin," John said. "We go through Lancaster. If you like, I could bring letters from your father."

"Would you?"

"Gladly."

"What are Praying Villages?" Libby asked.

"That's what we call the villages of Christian Indians. Our pastor in Roxbury learned their language and began preaching to them nearly thirty years ago. There are fourteen Praying Villages now."

"How exciting! What are the Indians like?" Libby asked. But John had no time to answer. Beside them Libby saw Father take a pen to sign the papers Zedekiah offered him. Below his signature she saw that of John's stepfather, Zedekiah Bassett.

"Let's go, John," he said. "You can help Jeremiah with his things. It will save time."

For the first time in her memory, Father hugged Libby tightly. "The Lord watch between me and thee while we are apart one from the other," he whispered.

"He will." Libby forced the words over the lump in her throat. She clung to the rail watching Father as he followed Mr. Bassett down the wharf. Once when he faltered, John took his arm. *Father's all right*, she told herself. *I can trust John to watch out for him.* When she could see Father no longer, she went below to gather her few belongings and wait for Mr. Rowlandson.

"Oh, Lord, take care of him," she whispered, throwing herself down on the straw pallet where she had slept for the past four months. Taking a deep breath, she reached for her winter cloak, intending to use it as a wrapper for her other belongings. Suddenly water spots dotted its surface. Libby shook her head vigorously, raking her wrist across her eyes.

Air refused to enter her blocked nose. Her whole body shook with each sobbing breath. She burrowed into the straw as far as she could, hoping no one else would come down.

"Libby, Libby Kendall!" someone called down the ladder hatch. "Are you ready to go? A man's here for you."

Libby sat up abruptly. Quickly she folded the cloak around her belongings, brushed the straw from her hair, and resettled her cap. Each step on the ladder required its own act of will, but too soon Libby reached the top.

If Mr. Rowlandson noticed her red eyes he said nothing. "Your father has gone?" he asked.

Libby nodded, not trusting her voice.

"I come to The Bay, as we call Boston, several times a year," Mr. Rowlandson said. "If he is near, you may send him a letter whenever I come."

"He's at Roxbury," Libby managed to say.

"I can deliver it easily, then." He glanced at Libby's awkward bundle. "Is this everything?"

"Yes, Sir." She smiled shakily.

"These are the papers you need to sign. You do read and write, don't you?"

"Yes." Libby read the articles carefully. They said she agreed to work four years for the Rowland- sons in payment for her passage. She signed her name neatly, then dated the signature: March 15, 1675.

"I'll carry your things," Mr. Rowlandson said. We go now to a family friend in Boston for the night. Tomorrow we shall start home. Hast thou ridden horseback?"

"No." In London only the rich rode horses. She and Father could not afford to travel farther than a day's walk.

"You'll soon get used to it. A carriage or even a wagon, for that matter, is impossible on our roads."

What could go wrong with a road? Libby won- dered, thinking of the cobbled streets of London. She soon found out. Away from the docks, many of Boston's streets remained unpaved. Holes of all sizes pocked the surfaces, some partly filled with gravel and water. "Ouch!" One foot dropped into an unexpected pothole. Sharp pains shot through Libby's ankle as it twisted. She bit her tongue to keep from crying out. After a few cautious steps the pain eased, but water saturated the bottom of her paper- soled shoe, nearly disintegrating it. After that, Libby watched her footing carefully.

She kept to the grass as they crossed Boston Commons. As they reached the middle, she saw a man in a pillory. He stood, his neck and head secured in a round hole. Other openings secured his hands so that he could not use them. Refuse thrown by passersby crusted his face and waistcoat. Libby's eyes shuddered away from him. She knew sinners must be punished, but she could never enjoy the sight. *If vengeance is God's as the Bible says, why don't men wait and let Him take it,* she wondered.

Mr. Rowlandson led her straight to the man. "Look at him girl, and learn the fate of those who leave the ways of righteousness."

Reluctantly Libby looked.   "Goodman Matthews!" she gasped.   "I'm so sorry! Was it you the constable took?"

"Elizabeth!" Mr. Rowlandson spoke sharply. "Do not speak to him. Don't you know that this man is a Quaker? God's wrath rests upon him."

"He saved my father's life," Libby said.

Mr. Matthews shivered in the chill air. But his face showed neither pain nor anger. His gray eyes held only love.

How could anyone do this? Angry tears burned her eyes.

"A godless Quaker!" Mr. Rowlandson said as they walked on.

"As covenant people, we cannot tolerate such evil! Remember Elizabeth, that Satan appears to us as an angel of light." He scowled fiercely. "The king forbids us to deal with them as they deserve, or we should soon be rid of them. Time was when we could have hanged them. Now we have to make do with the Cart and Whip Law."

Libby shivered. Good for the King! Perhaps he shared her thoughts about vengeance being God's alone. No one could persuade her Mr. Matthews was not a good man. They walked on in silence. She did not ask about the Cart and Whip Law. She did not want to know.

For a moment Libby forgot to watch where she put her feet. Suddenly warm manure squished around her soggy shoe soles. In front of her a grazing cow moved leisurely out of the way.

Once across the common, they passed tall clapboard houses, their second stories jutting over the street. Libby had begun to wonder how much longer

she could walk without limping when Mr. Rowlandson stopped at a whitewashed house and knocked.

Their hostess met them at the door. "This is
Libby Kendall," Mr. Rowlandson said. "She's the girl
who will help my wife." "Libby, this is Mistress
Bascomb." Mercifully he did not mention the en-
counter on the commons.

"Did you have a good journey?" Mistress Bascomb asked.

"Yes. We had some stormy weather, but only a
few days. I felt well for most of the trip."

"You traveled alone?"

"No. My father came with me. A merchant in
Roxbury bought his indentures." Libby fought un-
successfully to keep her voice from thickening at the
thought.

"And you just said good-bye to him. That's
enough to tire a body out even without the business
of getting your land legs back. What you need is rest.
You've a tiring trip ahead of you and work aplenty
when you get there."

Gratefully Libby followed Mistress Bascomb
through the carpeted living room to a steep ladder
to the second story. Through an open door she
caught a glimpse of the kitchen fireplace and the
eating board covered by a white cloth. She hadn't
expected such luxury in the New World. "Go on up,
Libby." Mistress Bascomb said. "There's a bed near
the chimney. You'll share it with Meg, our servant,
tonight. Sleep now if you can, Libby. We'll call you
for dinner."

After months on a straw pallet Libby had forgotten the luxury of a feather bed. She sank deep into
its softness and remembered nothing more until
dinner.

Chapter 2

Rowlandsons

Darkness still blanketed the town when Mistress Bascomb called Libby the next morning. Awkwardly Libby helped Mr. Rowlandson fit dried salted cod, loaf sugar, spices, a small packet of coffee, and her own meager possessions into a pack for one horse. A small noggin of molasses filled the other pack. Then he saddled the other horse and fastened the pillion behind the saddle. She eyed the unfamiliar cushion with its platform stirrup dubiously.

Mr. Rowlandson didn't seem to notice her discomfort. "Up you go," he said, offering her a helping hand. She perched awkwardly, clinging tightly to the back of the saddle.

As they crossed Boston Common Libby saw a cart hitched to two horses. It carried no load, but while she watched, the driver tied a man stripped to his waist behind it. Another man waited behind the tethered man, snapping a vicious-looking whip. "Hi-yup!" the driver shouted, urging the horses to trot. The other man's whip lashed sharply across the captive's back. Libby heard him cry out. As she watched, he stumbled.

Before he regained his footing the cart had dragged him several yards. Horrified, Libby watched the whip curl around his back again and again, cutting his skin to ribbons. She shuddered

convulsively. So that was what Mr. Rowlandson
had meant by the Cart and Whip Law! How could
a man survive more than a few miles of such treat-
ment?

In the morning dusk she could not see the man's
face. But a sudden fear stabbed her heart. Surely
Goodman Matthews had done nothing to deserve
this! Then as they crossed the common she recognized a hat lying crumpled on the ground. Goodman
Matthews had worn that hat the last time she and
Father spoke with him aboard ship.

Anger burned from her flushed cheeks to her
toes. She clamped her teeth over her lips to keep
from speaking. Ahead of her Master Rowlandson
paid no attention. She did not have to guess how he
would react if she spoke her thoughts. For the next
four years Master Rowlandson would control her life.
The thought left her shaking so hard she nearly lost
her handhold. *Lord, I don't want to be disrespectful
to my betters.* Libby tightened her grasp. *But I can't
believe Thou likest this.*

They lost sight of the cart when they turned onto
a side street and Mr. Rowlandson nudged the horse
into a trot. Keeping her seat on the pillion demanded
Libby's full attention.

Relief washed over her when Boston lay behind
them and Mr. Rowlandson slowed the horses. The
horses picked their way over a rutted road bordered
by small farms. Gradually her anger subsided leaving behind a sense of foreboding and a dull ache in
her heart. For the first time since they left the
common she noticed her surroundings. "Father and
I almost never left London," she forced herself to tell
Mr. Rowlandson. She must not show either fear or
anger. "I never knew what a farm looked like. And
I'd forgotten you could see so much sky at once on
land."

"We leave the farming area soon and enter the
forest," Mr. Rowlandson said pleasantly enough.

"You'll see genuine wild country before we reach home."

Nothing could be wilder than this road, Libby thought.   But Mr. Rowlandson's words promised adventure ahead.   "I can hardly wait," she said.

In midmorning the road narrowed to a rough trail, which wound beneath giant birch and oak trees, shutting out the March sun shining brightly overhead.   Never had she seen more than one or two trees at once.   They shut her in, smothering her with the unfamiliar damp odor.   Even in the open spaces between trees, she welcomed the warmth of her cloak.   "Those are azaleas," Mr. Rowlandson told her, pointing out a low bush.   "In a few weeks, every bush will be a splash of color along the path."   But for now leaf buds remained tightly folded on the bare trees overhead.

"This was once an Indian trail," Mr. Rowlandson explained.   "But we use it for the road to Lancaster."   He pointed to a boulder standing beside the trail.   "See the bowl-shaped depression on the top.   The Indians made it there so they could grind nuts when they were traveling."

He's trying to be kind, Libby thought, feeling a little better.   "Will we see Indians?"   she asked, remembering what John had told her about the Praying Indians.   John seemed to like them, but she couldn't help wondering about ordinary Indians.

"Probably not on the trail," Mr. Rowlandson said. We only see Indians when they want us to.   But you will see them often around Lancaster.   They're a simple people, basically friendly.   They're descended from the lost ten tribes of Israel, you know."

"Yes," Libby said.   "I read that about them in a tract when I was in London."

"Most of the time we get on well with the Indians," Mr. Rowlandson added.   "But when I was a boy our militia fought the Pequots."

When the sun stood overhead, Mr. Rowlandson guided the horses into a small clearing.   Libby stepped down, glad to put her feet on solid ground. She set out the cold corn bread and bacon Mistress Bascomb had sent with them. While she ate Libby propped herself against a sturdy tree, trying to sort out her troubled thoughts.

"What do you know of Massachusetts Bay Colony, Libby?" Master Rowlandson asked as he finished his corn bread.

"That it was founded as a haven for Puritans."

"Yes," Master Rowlandson said. "And it is here that we can live as God's covenant people, ruled by Him and our consciences. But we cannot forget that pure faith is always threatened. We have problems with heretics here, too, Libby."

"I'm not surprised," Libby said. "We had plenty of them in England."

Mr. Rowlandson continued. "To keep our covenant we have made strict laws. Quakers, for instance, teach anarchy and irreverence. We cannot and will not tolerate them here. We have had to expel other heretics as well. You may have heard of the Baptist Roger Williams. He now lives in Rhode Island, a neighboring colony. But men are not the only troublemakers." He looked at Libby sternly. "We were forced to deal harshly with Anne Hutchinson who dared set herself up against the church. On occasion we've applied the Cart and Whip Law to women, too."

Libby shivered. Perhaps Mr. Rowlandson had read her thoughts this morning. Was he warning her that she had transgressed already? Like all Puritans, she had learned in England how it felt to live as a dissenter. She had expected more mercy here. For the first time in her life, Libby dreaded the future. If she displeased the Rowlandsons they could turn her next four years into hell. *Surely I've nothing to worry about*, Libby told herself. *I'm satisfied to be a Puritan without being illegal.*

Lunch finished, Libby dragged herself up onto the pillion. All afternoon they wound through low hills, climbing, then dipping into miniature valleys. Several times Libby caught the glint of water through the trees. She longed to see a lake close up, but each time trees and bushes screened them from view.

By the time the sun hung low in the sky Libby's back ached. One foot had gone to sleep and she had hung on to the pillion for so long that she almost had to pry her fingers open before they would move. She began to wonder what it would feel like to fall off the horse.

At dusk Libby heard a clacking sound. Mr. Rowlandson guided the horse toward it into a muddy clearing. Ahead Libby saw a building.

"We'll spend the night at this inn," Mr. Rowlandson announced.

Inn? Libby thought. *Isn't this a stable?* Sliding to the ground, she stood staring, trying to locate the source of the noise. Vertical clapboards covered the cracks between the upended logs that formed the building's walls. Several had come loose and banged in the evening breeze. Libby made a face. Whoever built this place had not bothered with gravel or shrubbery either.

Inside, Libby forced herself to swallow a few bites of the watery porridge the innkeeper offered them, then slept soundly in spite of the lumpy straw tick he provided.

She woke next morning scratching bug bites. Age hadn't improved the porridge. She gulped it to avoid the taste, then followed Mr. Rowlandson outside. Ignoring her protesting muscles, she scrambled to her place, and they set off.

In late afternoon they came to a lake. "Except for the ocean that's the most water I've seen in one place," Libby told Mr. Rowlandson. Their trail followed the shore until the water narrowed to a river.

As the horses reached a small bridge they quickened their pace. "That's Lancaster," Mr. Rowlandson told her, pointing to the cluster of houses ahead. "Our house is across town on the hillside."

As they drew near the house Mr. Rowlandson pointed out, a door slammed and a boy a little younger than Libby raced out. "They're here!" A little girl appeared behind him, then a woman and a smaller girl. "Thank God you're here, Joseph," the woman said. "You're later than I expected. I was beginning to worry."

"It's a slower trip with loaded horses, Mary," Mr. Rowlandson said. "It's good to be home."

The boy came forward to help her down. To Libby's surprise, her legs refused to support her, and she crumpled to the ground in an undignified heap.

Mrs. Rowlandson ran to her. "Are you all right?" she asked.

"I-I think so," Libby said. "I'd never ridden before." Carefully she pulled herself to her feet.

"Come on in, child," Mrs. Rowlandson said. "Joseph, take her bundle."

A high-backed wooden settle stood in front of the hearth. Gratefully Libby collapsed onto the long hard bench and looked around her. One large fire room filled most of the downstairs. Only the braided rug beneath her feet relieved the bareness of the puncheon floor. Pegs fastened a "turn up" bedstead to the wall on one side of the fireplace. No doubt Master and Mistress Rowlandson slept there.

On the fireplace's other side pots and pans hung from pegs driven into the wall. A huge pot on legs stood over the fireplace coals, emitting a mouth watering fragrance. Trestles supported a narrow board at the end of the room.

While Mr. Rowlandson made introductions, Libby studied her new family closely. Five-year-old Sarah clung to her mother's skirt, staring, then as though she had made up her mind, she smiled and pulled herself onto the settle beside Libby. Mary, at ten, two heads shorter than Libby, asked, "Didst thou have a good ride? I always get tired riding pillion."

Joseph, who was fourteen, laughed. "How many times did you fall? Mary's always spilling."

"I didn't." Libby said. "But by the time we got here I was about to."

"Mary, you set the table for supper," Mrs. Rowlandson said briskly. "Sarah, baby, can you show Libby the way to the loft? Libby, there's a fresh straw tick at the head of the stair for you to sleep on. Put your things away and rest. You needn't begin work until we wash dishes after evening prayers."

Supper's fragrance kept its promise. Little Sarah sat beside her. "Have some more, Libby," she urged as Libby emptied her plate. Amused by her solicitude, Libby accepted Sarah's offers gratefully. When Mrs. Rowlandson wasn't looking, Libby slipped an arm around the little girl and hugged her. Sarah snuggled close. Libby's fears receded. *I'll love it here.*

The family gathered in front of the fireplace for prayers. Mr. Rowlandson lined out a familiar psalm, chanting each line for the family to sing after him. Then he read the nightly chapter from the Bible. Each family member, even little Sarah and last of all, Libby, took a turn praying. "I thank Thee," Libby said, "for traveling mercies, work, and a roof over my head—and be with Father." Guiltily she remembered she had scarcely thought of her father all day.

Next morning the unfamiliar sound of birds singing pulled Libby from sleep long before her body felt ready. For a moment she lay listening. Then, ignoring her protesting muscles, she pulled herself to her feet and donned her dark green work dress. She was halfway down the stairs when Mrs. Rowlandson came to the foot.

"Good morning, Libby. I was just ready to call you. Young Joseph is working in the fields with his father today, so there's wood to bring for heating wash water. You'll find the pile just outside the back door."

The house sat on a cleared hillside. Behind it the hill rose sharply. A little trail angled between stumps to the woodpile and the barn beyond. Behind the barn, trees and underbrush clothed the hilltop.

You're here to get wood, not explore, Libby reminded herself, turning from the waiting hill to the woodpile. When she loaded her arms, the downward slope made the return trip easier than she expected.

After a hearty breakfast (cornmeal porridge and molasses must be New England staples), Libby and Mrs. Rowlandson carried what seemed like endless buckets of water from the well to fill the big boiler over the fire. Ten-year-old Mary sorted the family laundry—stockings, breeches, and underwear that she called small breeches for Mr. Rowlandson and young Joseph. Libby added her wine-colored work dress, her petticoats and stockings to the women's clothing Mary sorted. Little Sarah sat on the hearth watching the water heat while she practiced her knitting. "We wash every month," Mary explained, "except in winter. Then we put it off longer. We've been saving it until you came." Libby smiled wryly.

Back in London a neighbor had warned her, "You'll work like a slave. Don't expect to shop at a market. Colonists make everything they need. You'll have no modern conveniences." Looking around the Rowlandson house, Libby had to admit life in their home at least, fulfilled the prediction.

While the water heated, Mr. Rowlandson and young Joseph joined them briefly for morning prayers.

They poured the hot water into a large tub in the yard. Mary carried more water inside and refilled the boiler. They would boil white garments, then cool them for scrubbing. Mistress Rowlandson returned to other household tasks, leaving Libby to scrub each piece by hand. The sun had dropped behind the trees when she spread the last of the wash across furniture backs and over pots on their wash across furniture backs and over pots on their pegs. The cold water and air had cracked Libby's hands. They throbbed as she warmed them over the fire. Her lips felt dry and cracked, too.

She glanced longingly at the settle, then turned to Mrs. Rowlandson. "How can I help with supper?"

Once she had eaten, Libby cleaned the cooking area. By then her eyelids sagged. It took all her willpower to stay awake during evening prayers. She added one hasty private prayer of her own as her head touched the pillow. "Please bless Father and help him with whatever he's doing," then slept deeply.

Chapter 3

Frontier Life

Libby and Mary spent the next day ironing and mending the clean clothing. Mrs. Rowlandson's busy feet kept the spinning wheel whirring. Sarah struggled valiantly with her knitting, trying to set the heel of a man's sock.

By dusk Libby's shoulders and eyes ached. Mrs. Rowlandson left the spinning wheel, lighted a pine knot torch, and set it on a flat stone in one corner of the fireplace. "You may take a few minutes to start stockings for yourself," she told Libby, handing her a ball of yarn.

"Thank you. Mine are nearly worn out." Libby scurried up the ladder for the knitting needles she had brought from England. Pulling a stool close to the torch, she set to work. Sarah brought her hornbook and sat on the hearth leaning against Libby's knees. "Do you want to see my sampler?" Mary asked, holding up her embroidery for Libby to admire.

"Good work," Libby said. *How good to have a family for company after a day's work*, she thought. *I'm glad I persuaded Father to come to New England.*

Even Mistress Rowlandson relaxed, smoking a pipe as she watched the roast turning over the fire. She had attached a leather thong to one end and fastened the thong's other end to the fireplace above

the fire. She twisted the thong tightly, then let it go.
As it unwound, the roast turned. When the thong
unwound completely, Mistress Rowlandson laid the
pipe down and retwisted it.

On Saturday they baked and cooked. Mistress
Rowlandson had warned Libby that no one cooked
on Sunday. *Even so, we'll eat well*, Libby thought as
Mistress Rowlandson outlined their work.

Libby lugged arm loads of dry "oven wood" and
lighted a fire in the brick oven on one side of the
fireplace. The wood burned fiercely. "You watch it,
Sarah," Mistress Rowlandson said, "and tell Libby
when it burns down. You can finish your sock at the
same time. You can stir the beans in the pot, too.
Mary, when you finish sweeping, there's wool to
card. Libby, you make bread, don't you?" Libby
nodded. "Good. You start it and I'll make a pumpkin
pie."

Libby scooped flour into a large bowl. "Where do
you keep the yeast?" she asked.

"Most of the time we don't have any," Mrs. Rowlandson said "You'll find the sour dough container
on the mantle."

Libby reached for the container and set it on the
board. "You'll have to tell me how much to put in.
I've used yeast more."

"Spoon in a bunch the size of your fist," Mrs.
Rowlandson told her.

Following Mistress Rowlandson's instructions,
Libby mixed milk, sourdough, lard, and salt into the
flour, then set the bread sponge on the hearth to
raise.

All morning Libby stoked the oven. "The oven's
ready," Mistress Rowlandson finally told her after the
noon meal. She checked the towel-wrapped loaves
raising on the hearth. "They're ready, too."

Thank goodness, Libby thought. She raked the
coals and ashes from the oven onto the heap on the
fireplace bed below.

"Mary, fetch the oak leaves and show Libby how to lay them in the oven," Mistress Rowlandson instructed.

"Doesn't she know?" Mary asked.

Libby shook her head. "What are they for?"

"We always put our loaves on leaves." Mary spread leaves on one side of the oven, then slid a loaf onto them. "In summer we use cabbage leaves because they're big. In the fall Sarah and I go aleafing so we'll have oak leaves to last the winter."

Amazed, Libby watched Mary. "I never saw anyone do that. In London we used pans. Thanks for showing me."

"Don't forget to close the chimney draft," Mistress Rowlandson warned.

By sundown baking smells filled the house. Libby loved the warm smell of molasses. Mistress Rowlandson used it in her baked beans and to sweeten the pie. Crusty loaves of bread and Mistress Rowlandson's pie cooled on the board where they ate. They left the bean pot hanging over the fire to stay as warm as possible.

Sabbath began Saturday at sundown. They stopped everything and Mr. Rowlandson conducted a double length prayer time. Afterward everyone went soberly to bed. Even the horses and oxen would rest tomorrow while their masters walked sedately to the meetinghouse in the center of Lancaster.

Libby's first Sunday in Lancaster dawned sunny, but cool. They ate breakfast silently, followed by a minimum of clearing up. Afterward the older children each fetched a Bible for personal prayers. At a nod from Mrs. Rowlandson, Libby followed their example. Sarah came to sit beside her. "Read to me, Libby."

Quickly, Libby turned to the story of the Good Samaritan and began to read aloud. "Thy family is like the Samaritan," she told Sarah when she finished. "They took me in when I needed a home."

"I thought you worked for us."

"I do," Libby said. "But a person always has to work somewhere. I'd rather do it here than anywhere I can think of."

"I'm glad you came, Libby," Sarah said, climbing onto her lap.

"You're the best little Samaritan of all." Libby hugged her.

"Sarah, get down." Mrs. Rowlandson said. "Libby is not allowed to spoil you."

For the first time in her life, Libby walked openly to Sunday meeting. Back home in London a small group of Puritans had met clandestinely in Father's shop. She had seldom gone to meeting anywhere else.

Here the meetinghouse dominated the town. As they walked she watched as other family groups converged from all directions. "I was glad when they said unto me: Let us go into the house of the Lord," Libby quoted joyously. Even the mounted wolf heads staring from the outside walls of the meetinghouse could not dampen her joy.

She tried to picture Roxbury in her mind. Father would be rejoicing, too, she knew. She felt suddenly lonely in spite of Sarah and Mary at her side.

Inside the meetinghouse she found a hard-packed dirt floor. Narrow, backless benches lined the sides with an aisle between. Men sat on one side, women on the other.

Because Mr. Rowlandson was the pastor, Mrs. Rowlandson and the girls sat on the front bench with their hand-carried foot warming stove. Young Joseph perched with the other boys on the steps leading to the pulpit. As an indentured servant, Libby did not sit with the family. She found her place in the back alongside the poor and other servants.

Libby joined the singing heartily. Pastor Rowlandson took his text from 1 Corinthians 5. The church must be purged, he said. She must be kept free from the workers of the enemy, such as Quakers.

They did not respect the Bible, God's Word. No one of the Elect, those God chose to save, would be drawn to them.

Libby thought again of Mr. Matthews. Would the enemy have led him to help her father? It couldn't be true! But what if she were deceived? Mr. Rowlandson thought so and he was a minister and a good man. Perhaps—blind terror paralyzed her at the thought—she was a reprobate—not Elect.

Libby's back began to ache. At the front she could see Sarah struggle valiantly not to fidget. *She's so little*, Libby thought. *Why couldn't she have a stool at her mother's feet like the other little girls?* Sarah, herself, had asked. But Mrs. Rowlandson had said Sarah must learn to endure hardness as a good little Christian.

Beside Sarah, Mary sat stiffly erect. As the sermon dragged on, Libby saw her grip the bench tightly, but she did not move.

At last the service ended. Sarah gave a happy little jump, only to have her mother slap her hands. Libby winced. She knew that Sarah could no more help jumping, than she could breathing.

Libby stood slowly, relishing the Sabbath quiet, then waited uncertainly for the family. "Do you feel well?" she asked Mary when the little girl reached the back. (She had ventured "thou" on Sarah, but Mary was old enough to demand respect for her position as mistress.)

"My head aches a little," Mary admitted. "It always does at meeting. And my hands are so cold I can't feel anything. You won't tell Mother, will you?"

"Of course not. It will be easier to sit when you get a little older. At least you have the foot warmer."

"Are you cold?" Mary asked.

"Of course," Libby said. "Everyone is. But we'll warm up soon."

Libby was glad to see a little color return to Mary's face in the fresh air outside. "You'll feel fine by the time we eat," she told the younger girl.

They lunched on bread, pie, and lukewarm beans. Then they all returned to the meetinghouse for afternoon meeting. When it ended at last, they walked home, shivering in the chilly air, to rest until the next day.

What choice do we have? Libby wondered. Mr. Rowlandson had explained that town ordinances forbade running, work, or any walking except to the meetinghouse. *Even resting is hard work here,* she thought, stifling a giggle at the idea. Maybe it should be against the rules, too.

Why do Lancaster's rules bother me? Libby wondered. In London they had followed rules equally strict; but there the rules came from God to Father, and she obeyed out of love to both. Here the rules seemed to come from a strange God, one to whom joy was a stranger. Libby stopped her thoughts just in time. If she could not control them, she would know God had rejected her. His chosen could surely control their thoughts.

At home the older Rowlandson children settled themselves around the hearth. Mary handed Libby a book. "We can read this on the Sabbath. Why don't you read it out loud?"

Libby looked at it closely. "*The Saint's Everlasting Rest,*" she read from the cover and turned to chapter one. When at last the sun went down, she put away the book and went outside to carry water. Sabbath had ended and Libby had to wash dishes.

Monday dawned stormy. Cold winds howled out of leaden skies as they deposited a skim of snow along the already frozen path. Returning from the woodpile, Libby slipped, turning the same ankle she had twisted in Boston. It had not swollen then, but it had never lost a sore feeling when she stepped on it. By the time she brought in the third load of wood, it had bulged alarmingly over her shoe.

Libby stared at her ankle in dismay. *I can't sit down now,* she thought. *I'm here to work, not to be a burden.* She deposited the wood on the stack in the corner and hopped her way up the stairs, hoping Mrs. Rowlandson wouldn't notice. There must be something I can bind it up with. If only she hadn't left her worn-out handkerchiefs and linens in London.

Tearing her only good handkerchief into strips, she bound the offending ankle so tightly that it throbbed worse than ever. She let her weight down gingerly. It hurt, but if she went carefully, she could walk on it.

"Libby," Mrs. Rowlandson called. "Where are you? I thought you were going to help Mary fetch wood."

"I am," Libby answered. "I just had to get a handkerchief." She edged her way cautiously back down the narrow ladder.

Somehow Libby managed most of her work without anyone noticing her ankle. But once she caught Mrs. Rowlandson looking at her. Libby sighed. *She thinks I'm dawdling, but I can't help it*, she thought. She gritted her teeth and moved a little faster.

By evening prayers Libby could no longer hide her pain. She propped her leg on a footstool during Bible reading. When everyone else knelt to pray she didn't move.

"Libby, are you ill?" Mrs. Rowlandson asked when they finished.

Libby shook her head. "No, Ma'am, just a little tired." She pulled herself to her feet and hopped toward the ladder to the second story.

"Have you hurt yourself, child?"

She must not lie. "My ankle is a little sore. I slipped on the path."

"When did that happen?" Mrs. Rowlandson asked sharply.

"This morning."

"Let me see that foot."

Libby sank back into the chair gratefully. "I can do it myself," she protested when Mrs. Rowlandson began to unwrap the awkward bandage. But she did not move.

Beneath the stocking Libby's ankle puffed, angry red and purple. Mrs. Rowlandson gasped. "Why didn't you say something?"

"I had work to do."

"Well, tomorrow you can sit down to card wool and spin. Right now let's get hot compresses on that ankle. Do you think you can sleep on the hearth for a night or two?"

"Yes, Ma'am." Libby sighed with relief as Mrs. Rowlandson and Mary applied the hot compresses. She had survived today. Tomorrow could take care of itself. Mrs. Rowlandson would find out soon enough that she had never carded wool or spun in her life.

Libby worked her way slowly down the ladder the next morning. What would Mistress Rowlandson think when she discovered that Libby did not know how to spin?

"You can make porridge this morning," Mistress Rowlandson told her. Libby took her place on the settle gratefully.

The porridge lumped. The adults and young Joseph ate it silently, and Libby forced hers down. Sarah whined.

"Don't you know how to make porridge?" Mary asked, sounding superior. "You have to put the cornmeal in a little at a time."

Libby grinned wryly. "I didn't know," she said, "but I do now and I'll never forget."

"I thought everybody knew how to make porridge."

Libby didn't answer. After Libby succeeded in washing the dishes sitting down, Mrs. Rowlandson called her to the spinning wheel. Libby hopped across the room.

"I never used one in London," she admitted.

"Mary can help you get started," Mrs. Rowlandson said. With a sore foot, Libby found it hard to keep the wheel moving at even speed.

Mary watched her closely. She seemed to take a perverse pleasure in correcting Libby. "How come you never spun?" she asked finally. "Only rich people don't have to spin."

"I wasn't rich," Libby snapped. "Do you think I'd be an indentured servant if I were? We had shops in London! Even poor people could buy yarn and yard goods."

Mary stared at her. "Really?" she asked, but Libby could tell Mary didn't believe her.

"I don't lie!" Libby said before she could stop herself. "I'm sorry," she added contritely.

Mistress Rowlandson intervened. "Libby's right, Mary. London is settled country—not like here."

By lunch time Libby had achieved a small ball of good yarn, but frustration tightened every muscle in her body. Why couldn't Mary leave her any peace? Libby felt like screaming.

She slopped hot water on one hand when she prepared to wash dishes, but she managed to finish them and hobble to the back porch with the water. Without looking, she flung it viciously into the back yard.

"Ow!" someone yelled.

Chapter 4

Ishmael

Libby jumped and peered toward the bushes. What had she done now? What looked at first like a dripping black mop stepped into view. It shook the dripping hair from its face and strode toward the door. Libby clung to the casing, staring. "You scared me to death! Did I drown you?"

"I guess not. It's about the welcome I should have expected from Mr. Rowlandson." The boy looked about her age—dark-haired with eyes and skin to match, slim, with high cheek bones. The bitterness of his voice erased her own frustrations from Libby's memory.

"I'm sorry," she repeated. "I had no idea you were out there."

"Or even that I existed, I daresay. For that matter, who are you?"

"I'm Libby Kendall, the-the indentured servant."

The boy shivered. "The name is Ishmael Brown. Mistress Rowlandson's sister is my foster mother. Now, may I go in, or would you rather I turned into an icicle?"

Libby flushed. "Go in, of course," she said, suddenly contrite.

"After you." He bowed, dripping dirty water across her white apron.

Forgetting her foot, Libby took a quick step forward. "Oh!" She steadied herself against the table. Ishmael paid no attention. When the pain subsided she hopped back to the settle.

"Why Ishmael, you look like a drowned rat!" Mistress Rowlandson said. "Whatever happened? I thought it was too cold to rain."

"I was attacked by angry dishwater."

On the settle, Libby tried to make herself as small as possible. She picked up the wool cards again. Would he never go?

....

"Libby?" She jumped at the sound of Mary's voice.

"Yes?" Libby's hands maintained a steady rhythm.

"Did you really dump dishwater on Ishmael, or did he make it up?"

"I really did," Libby said. "But it was an accident. I was sorry."

To her surprise, Mary laughed. "I've wanted to do something to him so many times, but I don't dare."

"Why?" Libby asked.

"Ishmael's mean. Didn't you see him pull Sarah's hair?"

"No. I was trying not to look at him."

Mary sighed. "I guess it's no more than you'd expect of a bastard."

So that was Ishmael's problem. His parents had never been properly married. As a bastard his social position was as low as her own. And for him there was no escape. It explained the undercurrent of bitterness she had sensed when he spoke.

By the next day, Libby's ankle could bear a little weight. With Mary's help, she achieved a pot of unlumpy porridge, and she managed to limp through most of her regular tasks. She almost forgot Ishmael.

That evening someone knocked on the Rowland-son door. When Mary let Ishmael in, she jumped out of his reach. Mistress Rowlandson frowned.

Ignoring both of them, Ishmael sped across the room to the settle where Libby sat knitting, and plopped down beside her. "You aren't really mad about what I said, are you, Libby?"

For the first time, she looked at him directly. His restless eyes and hands never stopped moving. "I guess not. But I thought I'd die when you told Mistress Rowlandson about the dishwater. She never said a thing to me afterward, though."

Ishmael laughed. "She probably thought I deserved it. At any rate she wouldn't believe anything I said. She thinks I'm the devil's own."

Libby looked at him sharply. "Are you?"

The mocking laughter died. "I-I don't know."

"What do you want to be?"

Ishmael stared at his clenched fists. "I don't know," he repeated. "But it doesn't matter. I was born what I am. Now I suppose you hate me, too."

The bitterness in his voice brought sudden tears to her eyes. "Why should I?" she asked softly. "I'm the one who drowned you, remember? And you're honest. I like that."

Ishmael sat fidgeting for a moment; then, abruptly, he spoke. "Did they tell you who I am?"

"Only that you're a bastard. Does it matter so much?"

"Yes. My parents wanted to get married, but my father was an Indian. After they tied my mother to a cart and whipped her through town, they made a label of shame for her to wear on one sleeve. They whipped my father, too, and forbade him to come back. His family lived at Nashobah, the Praying Village. Praying Indians wouldn't let him stay there, either. When I was born my mother died. So you see to them I'm not even a charity case. I'm a walking reminder of the wages of sin."

Abruptly Ishmael stood up. "Your sister said to tell you she'd like to borrow molasses, Mistress Rowlandson," he said. "She'll pay you back when my foster father gets home from The Bay."

He paced the floor while Mistress Rowlandson poured a cup of molasses. When she handed it to him, he stalked to the door, yanking Sarah's braid as he passed. Sarah whimpered. Mr. Rowlandson opened his mouth to say something, but Ishmael slammed the door before he could get it out.

Libby stared after the boy thoughtfully. Beside Ishmael's hurt, four years of virtual slavery seemed like nothing. She had Mary and little Sarah. He had no family and, she suspected, no friends either—no future but shame. *I like him,* she thought, surprised. *But I don't know if he wants friends.*

By Saturday Libby worked as usual, although the ankle felt sore and tender. She was debating whether or not she could walk to the meetinghouse, when someone knocked. Libby answered the door. Ishmael stood outside tracing lines in the mud with a long stick.

"I brought you this," he said. Wiping mud off the end, he held out a polished stick with a carved top. "I figured you'd want to go to meeting."

Libby smiled at the sight of the walking stick. "Thanks. I had almost decided I couldn't walk that far, but now I'll be fine." She leaned her weight on the stick. "This is beautiful. Did you make it?"

For once Ishmael seemed embarrassed. "Yes. Thank you," he mumbled, then asked, "How did you hurt your ankle?"

"I was attacked by an angry path," Libby said, laughing. Ishmael laughed with her.

"I twisted it first, in a pothole in Boston," Libby explained. "Then last week I slipped on the path."

The next day at Meeting Libby spotted Ishmael perched with young Joseph and the other boys on the pulpit steps. In spite of herself, she watched him.

Ishmael sat stiffly erect, his eyes apparently fixed on Mr. Rowlandson. Although he never moved, there was no stillness in him. After Mr. Rowlandson's final "amen," Ishmael shot through the narrow aisle like a released spring.

Libby waited until most of the crowd had left before she stood up. "I'll walk with you," Sarah offered, and her mother smiled approval.

When they reached the rutted street, Ishmael fell in step with them. "Hello," he said to Libby, snatching a fistful of Sarah's hair.

"Ouch!" Sarah yelled.

Libby glared at him. "You can stop that right now, Ishmael Brown, if you want to walk with me."

"All right." But Ishmael showed no sign of repentance.

"Why do you pester Sarah?" Libby asked.

Ishmael looked at her, surprised. "I don't know. Just teasing, I guess."

"But it's cruel."

"No, it's not. It teaches Sarah to face life."

"You think life is cruel?"

"Don't you? If you weren't an indentured servant, you would be everybody's sweetheart."

"I don't want to be anybody's sweetheart!" Libby protested, then blushed, remembering John. If only Roxbury were closer.

"You'll change your mind," Ishmael said. "And when you do, I'm qualified."

"Not if you persist in pulling Sarah's hair."

Ishmael grinned. "I'm a reformed individual. You really are pretty, Libby. It's a good thing I have four years before the rest of the world discovers you."

Libby laughed, then looked around quickly to make sure no one had noticed her unsabbathlike behavior. She blushed. "That's what you think! I'm not invisible, you know."

"You don't understand indentures, do you?"

Ishmael walked her home again after the afternoon service. "Guess I'd better stay 'til sundown," he told her, grinning. "Can't have any excess walking on the Sabbath."

"Of course not," Libby agreed, smothering a giggle. She hoped Mistress Rowlandson didn't notice.

Ishmael strolled inside confidently. "Hello little one." He made a face at Sarah and stuck his hands into his pockets ostentatiously.

"We want Libby to read to us," Mary informed him.

"I will," Libby said quickly.

"I'll listen then," Ishmael said, staring at her until she could feel the blood rush to her face.

"Why don't you take a turn?" Libby asked softly as she reached the halfway mark in her chapter.

A spasm of pain crossed his face. "Why should I? It's only interesting when I can watch you." She glared at him and went on reading, but she could not forget that split second of pain.

"Is something wrong, Ike?" she asked when the chapter ended. "Does your head ache?"

"Of course not. Where'd you get that name for me?"

"I made it up. I'm not sure I like Ishmael. The Bible says Ishmael's hand was against every man, and you try too hard to live up to that."

Ishmael only stared at her.

"You didn't answer my question," Libby said. "Does your head ache? You looked like you hurt when I asked you to read."

"I'm lazy." Ishmael said. "I avoid all intellectual pursuits."

"Nonsense! But something's wrong. Can I help? After all that dishwater I owe you a good turn."

"It's like I said. I'm lazy. My foster mother wants to educate the bad blood out of me. She wants me to be a minister—says it will make up for my mother's sins. But my Latin stops with *agricola* and I never read unless I have to."

Libby laughed softly. "You a minister? I think not! You were made for outdoor work. The frontier is a perfect place for you."

Ishmael stared at her. "None of it matters to you, does it?"

"Of course not. My father is a cordwainer. No pastor could be more God's man than he is making shoes."

The belligerence melted from Ishmael's face. "I'm not like that, Libby," he said softly.

"I know," Libby said. "And it pains me. But you're not lazy."

"I can plow a field," Ishmael said. "Or work for weeks cutting timber, and I don't mind at all. But give me one chapter to read!" He rolled his eyes and moaned.

"Do you have trouble reading?"

Ishmael wouldn't look at her. "Yes," his lips framed.

"Maybe if we read together—"

"You can't cure bad blood."

"What does blood have to do with it? You're not stupid. Mistress Rowlandson has told me of Indians going to Harvard, so that's no excuse. When I was on the ship I taught some of the other girls to read." She laid her hand gently on his shoulder. "Do your foster father or Mr. Rowlandson know?"

Ishmael nodded. "I have the scars to show it. The good pastor beat me more than once before he gave up."

"He'd want you to try. I'm sure he'll let us do it. And I've never beaten anyone in my life."

Ishmael jumped to his feet. "No. But you can sure drown a guy." He laughed—this time without mockery. "I'm willing to try. But I'd lay odds they'll tell you not to speak to me again."

"Elizabeth," Mr. Rowlandson said after Ishmael had left. "I think I should warn you about Ishmael. Not only is he a bastard of mixed blood, he is a rebel and has no concern for his soul."

"I knew the first part," Libby said. "But I'm not sure about the last. He's honest, and underneath, he might care."

"What has the boy been saying to you?"

"About the same thing you just said."

Mr. Rowlandson stared at her. "He did?"

"He's willing to read with me if you'll let us. I know he cares about that," she continued.

"I-I don't know what to say," Mr. Rowlandson said. "I feel responsible to God and your father for your welfare."

"Let her try, Joseph," Mistress Rowlandson said. "The boy has never had a friend, and Libby does seem to bring out the best in him. My sister is at her wit's end."

Mr. Rowlandson frowned. "Very well, Libby. You have my permission to try. But don't expect much. Anytime I see evidence that his rebellious attitude is influencing you, lessons will stop." He paused, then smiled. "I noticed he let Sarah alone tonight. Did you have a hand in that?"

"It's the only way I would speak to him."

"Confine your teaching to evening hours. Summer work will be upon us before we know it."

"Yes, Sir. Thank you."

Ishmael returned in the evening a few days later, bringing a cup of molasses for Mistress Rowlandson. He gave it to her, and turned to Libby. "At your service, Ma'am. My father asked me to deliver this letter."

As she unfolded the paper, a smaller piece fell to the floor. Ishmael retrieved it and turned it over in his hand. "What's that?" Libby asked.

"Oh, nothing."

"Then you won't mind letting me see it, will you?"

Ishmael looked sullen. "It's only a scrap."

Like a flash Libby's hand shot out and snatched the paper. Ishmael glared.

Libby ignored him and studied the paper in her hand. It contained a brief note. "Dear Libby, Your father gains strength slowly. I expect to pass through Lancaster with Daniel Gookin in May. With your permission, I shall call on Rowlandsons in the hope of seeing you. John Morris."

Quickly Libby stuffed the note in her apron pocket and turned to the longer letter. Father's familiar script filled the page. "My dear daughter: All goes well. The Bassetts are a fine family. Zedekiah's main business comes from selling imported merchandise. But he is anxious to set up a cordwainer's shop with my help. You will be glad to know that his stepson, John, assists with accounting as his studies permit. I trust you are well and happy. Your Father, Jeremiah Kendall."

"Good news?" Mistress Rowlandson asked as Libby smiled. "Yes. My father is doing well. His letter sounds happy." Libby turned to Ishmael. "What did you think you were doing when you grabbed that paper?" she demanded.

"I thought you were my friend," Ishmael said so low no one else could hear. "We're both alone. That gives me a right."

"I can have more than one friend at a time," Libby told him. "As for being a friend, you're making a bad start. And speak for yourself about being alone. If you'd give anyone a chance you wouldn't be alone, either."

Ishmael stared at her for a long moment. "I did try." He seemed to choke on the words. "But it doesn't matter. I'll make you my sweetheart. You'll see." Ishmael strode to the door, banging it behind him.

Mistress Rowlandson sighed. "You never know what that boy is going to do! I fear for him."

Libby's anger began to cool. *I do, too*, she thought. *Why should he be jealous? I don't want a sweetheart until my four years are up. And at any rate, I scarcely know John.*

Nevertheless, when Libby dressed the next morning, she left John's note in the bottom of her apron pocket where she had put it the night before.

She was surprised that evening when Ishmael came to the door. "Your sister sent me to see Libby," he told Mistress Rowlandson sullenly.

Libby picked up her Bible. "Here I am. Want to read?"

"You've been talking about me."

"Mr. Rowlandson brought up the subject. I only told him you cared about reading—and a lot of other things."

Ishmael grimaced. "I can imagine what he said." He hesitated. "Thanks, Libby. Guess we have to give it a try. But the leopard can't change his spots. That's in the Bible, isn't it?"

"Yes. But it also says, 'I will take away your heart of stone and give you a heart of flesh.'"

"You win. From henceforth I'm a model student."

Libby opened her Bible to the parable of the Prodigal Son. "Here's a good starting point."

Ishmael had told the truth. Reading came hard. He labored painfully to make out each word. An hour passed while they followed the son through his years of riotous living to near starvation in the pig sty, then home to his father.

At the end, Ishmael slammed the Bible shut and grabbed her wrist. "Trying to preach to me?"

"Not really. It's a good story."

Ishmael tightened his grip. "Well, I haven't been anywhere, and I'm not crawling home."

"Maybe not. But I often think the Rowlandsons' pigs are happier than you are."

He released Libby's wrist abruptly. "I can't help who I am."

"I'm sorry, Ike." Libby took a deep breath. "I like who you are."

"I'll be back, Libby Kendall. And I'll read if it's the last thing I ever do."

"It won't be."

"I'll hold you to that promise."

Ishmael walked to the door, opened it, and slipped out with exaggerated slowness.   Cold air rushed into the fire room as the door slid shut gently.

Ishmael arrived the next night whistling cheerfully.   "I brought you something," he told Libby, handing her a small dish.   "My mother wants the dish back."

Libby carried the dish to the table and transferred its contents to one of Mistress Rowlandsons'. "Molasses taffy!   Thank you.   I haven't had sweets since—since Mother died.   Bring your candle in here, Ike.   It's a good place to study."

Libby selected a shorter parable for the night's lesson.   But halfway through Ishmael slammed the Bible on the table.   "It's no use.   I knew it wouldn't get easier."

"I think I see why," Libby said.   "You keep having to start over.   Once you have a word figured out you forget it before you see it again."

"I told you it's hopeless," Ishmael said.

"Let's try something different.   Next time draw the letters with your finger while you spell it out."

"What good will that do?"

"What harm will it do?" Libby asked.

To her own surprise the idea worked.   After two or three tracings while he spelled out a word, Ishmael remembered.   Before he left for the night Ishmael was able to read the first two verses fluently.

Chapter 5

Teacher

No sooner had Ishmael shut the door than young Joseph sat down beside Libby at the table. "Libby has a beau!" he announced.

Libby flushed. "Of course not! I'm only helping him read."

"Do you have any idea how much my aunt hates to make taffy? If he didn't like you, he wouldn't even dare ask."

"That will be enough, Joseph," Mr. Rowlandson said. "Libby is only doing her Christian duty."

Libby pushed the candle as far away as she could reach, hoping the dim light hid her face. "Get out your knife, Joseph. You can divide it between all four of us."

Joseph divided the two pieces into four equal portions.

Ishmael did not return the following evening. "I knew he wouldn't stick with it," Master Rowlandson said. "Your efforts are in vain, Elizabeth."

Two nights later Libby saw Ishmael crossing the yard. Before he could knock, Mr. Rowlandson opened the door. "Where have you been?" he demanded. "You come to study, not to call on Elizabeth."

Fidgeting, Ishmael looked at Mistress Rowlandson as though seeking an ally. "My foster mother sprained her arm," he said sullenly. My foster father spends all day in the fields, and his son has to study for college. I couldn't leave."

"Is it better now?" Mistress Rowlandson asked.

"A little. She can't do much, but she made me come anyway."

"You can tell her I'll send Libby over tomorrow," Mistress Rowlandson said.

"Let me go, too," Sarah begged.

"What can you do to help?" Mr. Rowlandson asked.

Sarah thought a moment. "I can talk to her so she won't get lonely while Libby works."

Mr. Rowlandson smiled. "A thoughtful idea, Sarah. If Elizabeth wishes, she may take you."

"Of course you can come," Libby said. "I need you to show me the way."

She and Ishmael cut the evening lesson short, but to Libby's delight, Ishmael remembered the words he had traced earlier. "Tell your mother I'm looking forward to seeing her," she told Ishmael as he left.

No light showed through the wall chinks when Libby and Sarah crawled from their beds the next morning. By leaving before sunup they could reach Mistress Kerley's home in time to prepare breakfast there.

Sarah clung to Libby's hand as they started down the still shadowy path. As the day brightened she let go to skip ahead. "Stay in sight," Libby warned her, "or I won't know where to turn." Most of the time Sarah obeyed, but once she vanished around a curve. Moments later Libby heard her call. "Libby! Libby!" Before Libby could answer, Sarah ran, stumbling, into view. When Libby held out her arms, the little girl catapulted into them, wrapping her legs around Libby's waist.

"What is it?" Libby asked, wincing from the strength of Sarah's grip. "You're choking me, Sarah."

"There's an Indian up there," Sarah snuffled.

Libby's heart pounded, but she kept her voice steady. "What was he doing?"

"Just walking. Walking to my aunt's house."

"The path is for everybody, Sarah. He can walk on it if he wants to." Libby forced herself to walk forward without hesitating. *Mr. Rowlandson said they've been friendly for years,* she reminded herself. But why would one go to Mistress Kerley's house? Perhaps Sarah had his destination wrong.

They came to a clearing and a two-story house. Sarah turned her head to look, then buried her face in Libby's shoulder. "He's here!"

Ahead of them Libby saw one of the tallest men she had ever seen. Around his waist he wore a wrapped cloth fastened in back and front to form a sort of breeches. Leather leggings encased his legs. Beneath the large fur slung cape-style over one shoulder, Libby glimpsed a ruffled shirt such as English gentlemen wore. Grease glistened from any exposed skin. Looking at his paint-daubed face, Libby understood Sarah's fear.

The Indian called, and Ishmael bounded out the door. To Libby's surprise he greeted the man in a language she had never heard. The Indian put down a pack of furs. Ishmael darted into the house and returned with a basket of his trading goods.

Libby stroked Sarah's hair with one hand. "It's all right, Sarah. He came to trade furs with Ishmael." With Sarah still clinging to her, Libby strode briskly across the yard.

Ishmael smiled when he saw her. "Hello, Libby. This is my friend, Wusassmon."

Lowering Sarah to the ground, Libby held out her hand. What did you say to an Indian? "Pleased to meet you," she said. The Indian smiled. "How do you do?" he asked in careful English. Libby's fear vanished. In spite of the paint, he was only an ordinary person conducting business. Behind her she heard the door squeak as Sarah snatched it open, and plunged inside.

Libby found her nestled on Mistress Kerley's lap. "It's good to have you, Libby," Ishmael's foster mother said. "There, there, Sarah. An Indian is nothing to fear."

"They give me nightmares," Sarah said. She stayed close to her aunt most of the morning. When they walked home that evening she stayed close to Libby's side.

By April's end the weather warmed slightly. One night when Ishmael came to read with Libby he announced: "Azaleas are blooming."

"I want to see them," Mary said. "Mother, if we finish all our work early tomorrow, can't Libby and I take Sarah to the woods."

"I want to see good quality work," Mistress Rowlandson said severely.

"That means we can go!" Smiling, Mary bounced toward Libby. "I can hardly wait. Don't worry, Mother. You've never seen better work than I'll do tomorrow."

All the next morning Libby cleaned and carried firewood, thinking of the promised outing. Mary thumped away rhythmically at the spinning wheel, teeth clamped over her lower lip in concentration. Not to be outdone, Sarah trotted through the house swiping at everything she could reach with a dust cloth.

"You have done well," Mistress Rowlandson said at noon. "At two-thirty you may go."

In midafternoon Libby folded the last carefully ironed pillowcase and set the flatiron on the mantle to await its next use.

Mary tugged at Libby's arm. "Hurry! We're almost ready." Libby climbed the stairs and took her hood from its peg.

"Come on!" Mary called. "You don't need many wraps. It feels like summer out." Hastily Libby settled the hood in place and tied her kerchief shawl around her shoulders.

"Don't go too far," Mistress Rowlandson warned them. "And Mary and Sarah, stay out of the mud."

The forest began halfway up the hill behind the house. As they entered, tree branches closed over the path behind them, shutting out everything except the green of the young leaves and the soft twitter of birds in the trees ahead of them. Sarah took Libby's hand. "I'm glad you're here, Libby. I get scared in the woods."

Libby stopped, letting the silence sink into her. "I know, Sarah," she whispered. "I feel like an intruder, too."

"Why?" Mary asked. "They're our woods."

"Are they? Look around. They're just like God made them. They've been here for thousands of years with nobody to bother them but Indians."

Libby walked slowly, admiring each unfamiliar leaf and blossom. Suddenly Sarah's grip tightened convulsively. "Libby, who's there?"

Beside the path ahead the bushes parted. Libby's heart pounded. Were there Indians here? Then a face appeared, grinning.

Libby did not smile back. "Ishmael Brown! What are you up to? You scared us to death!"

"Serves you right for talking such nonsense, Libby. These are white man's woods. Anyone can tell."

"How?"

"By the undergrowth. The Indians keep it burned off. It makes better hunting, they say."

Libby's heart resumed normal speed. "Let's go, girls." She squeezed Sarah's hand reassuringly.

Ishmael fell in step ahead of Libby on the narrow path. "Just ahead we'll find dogwood in bloom," he told them.

When they reached the dogwood tree Mary stopped. "I want flowers to take home."

"Pick away." Ishmael grinned cheerfully.

"But I can't reach."

"Then climb." Ishmael turned his back, whistling.

Libby stood on tiptoe grasping a branch. "I can pull it down. You and Sarah pick."

When the girls had filled their arms, Libby stepped in front of Ishmael, blocking his way. "What did you mean by that?"

"No use pampering them. In this country you have to take care of yourself."

Libby glared at him. "Does that preclude common manners?"

"Maybe not." Ishmael dragged his toe along the ground. "I never thought about it."

Beside them the underbrush crackled. "What's that?" Mary asked. Before anyone could answer, a pup burst onto the path and planted joyful paws against Ishmael's woolen stockings. Ishmael kicked him loose.

"It's all right, boy," Libby stooped to comfort the bewildered puppy. He slunk under her skirts until all she could see were two brown eyes regarding Ishmael warily.

It was Ishmael's turn to look bewildered. "I thought you approved of manners."

"I do," Libby said. "But he doesn't know why you punished him. How can he learn?"

"He can't," Ishmael said. "But it's the way to keep him under control. At any rate dogs are used to it."

"Not where I come from." A street cur had appeared at their door in London, frightened and cringing like the pup. It had taken Libby weeks to win his confidence, and more weeks to make him understand instructions. But at the last he had obeyed her joyously. Her heart still twisted guiltily when she remembered abandoning him to the streets when they left London. But she could find no home for him.

Libby shook the burning tears from her eyes. "Let's go back, girls." The puppy followed her to the dooryard, then sat staring hopefully at the house. She gave him a quick hug before she went in.

The smell of roasting meat greeted Libby as she entered the house. Mistress Rowlandson turned from the fireplace where she was turning beef on a spit. "You're back in good time. You take over, Libby. I'll start corn cakes. Mary, there are dried apples soaking in the small pot. Will you hang it over the fire?"

A knock at the door interrupted their work. "You answer it, Sarah," Mistress Rowlandson said. Libby smiled, watching Sarah put on adult dignity as she reached the door. "Can I help you?" she asked primly.

"May I speak to your mother, Miss? I am hoping she will permit me a word with Miss Libby Kendall."

Sarah beckoned, smiling. "Come in. Mama, Libby, he wants to see you."

John stood taller than she remembered. He waited, feet apart. *How solid he looks. Nothing could budge him unless he chose to move,* Libby thought. She turned her face back to the roast, glad that the blazing fireplace made a reason for her burning cheeks.

"My name is John Morris." he told Mistress Rowlandson. "Libby's father is my friend. I promised him that I would stop to see her."

"Libby, do you know this man?"

"Yes. He was at the ship when his stepfather bought my father's indentures."

"Didn't she tell you about me?" John asked.

Libby flushed. "What's to tell?" She fished the note from her apron pocket and handed it to Mistress Rowlandson. "He sent me this with Father's letter. I meant to tell you, but Ishmael made such a fuss about it, I couldn't bring myself to say anything."

Mistress Rowlandson smiled. "I can understand that. Come in, John. You're welcome to talk to Libby."

The spit turned ever faster under Libby's hand. *What can I say?* She had composed dozens of mental replies to John's note, but seeing him chased every word from her memory.

"You're a welcome sight, Libby." John said. "This place agrees with you."

"If Father were only near I'd be perfectly happy. How is he?"

"He seems to feel well but he is not strong. My stepfather set him to making boots, and I made sure that his work area is near a fireplace. I also told my mother to try and fatten him up."

"I prayed you'd watch out for him, John. He doesn't know how much looking after he needs."

"He's helped me, Libby. I'd never thought what it would mean to stand up for what you believe when the laws of the land went against you. I don't know if I'll ever match his courage, but I'm learning. Now, what about you?"

"I love it here. Naturally Mistress Rowlandson is strict, but I like her. I haven't had a woman I could talk to since my mother died. And I love the girls. I never had brothers or sisters for long. All the babies died."

"How long ago did your mother die?"

"When I was thirteen."

John smiled. "And you've been looking out for your father ever since?"

"We'd have starved if I hadn't. As it was we left one jump ahead of debtors' prison."

John took the handle of the spit from her. "It was like that with us when I was little. After my father died, Mother sewed and scrubbed for anyone who needed her. I was too small to help much. Most of the time we had enough money for cornmeal, but nothing else." He laughed. "My stepfather used to give her a special price for cornmeal and molasses. That's how they got acquainted."

"What about your stepfather?" Libby asked. She couldn't imagine Father remarrying.

"Sometimes I forget he's not my real father, and so does he. He'd like me to take over his business."

"Will you?"

John shook his head. "No. I can do accounts, but it's people I want to work with."

"Then you'll be a minister?"

"Yes. But more than that, I hope."

"What do you mean?"

"What this country needs is doctors—real doctors who know the latest developments in medicine."

Libby inserted a fork into the meat. "The roast is done," she told Mistress Rowlandson.

"I'll take care of it. You and Mary dish up the other food. You will stay for dinner, won't you, Mr. Morris?"

"I would be pleased, Ma'am."

As she set the platter of corn cakes on the table Libby couldn't help smiling. Sarah had already set an extra place.

Libby stood at the back door, dishpan in hand when Ishmael came whistling along the path over the hill. When he saw her he stopped, covered his head with his hands, hunched his shoulders, then tiptoed down the path.

Libby laughed. "You're safe, Ike." She splashed the water against a nearby bush. "Come on in. I'll be with you in a minute."

Inside the house Mr. Rowlandson made introductions. "A pleasure to meet you," Ishmael said. But his words sounded like a challenge.

"I read with Ishmael in the evenings," Libby explained to John. "We relax that way."

"I see." John sounded as upset as Ishmael. Libby stared from one to the other. What was the matter with them? A few minutes later John excused himself and left.

She set Ishmael a passage that they had read before. He had never done so well. "If that's what John does to you, he ought to stay around," she whispered.

Ishmael swore under his breath. "He'd soon wish he hadn't," he said.

He slammed the door as it had not slammed in weeks.

Puzzled, Libby stared after him.

Libby was gathering eggs the next morning when she heard Ishmael come whistling up the path. "Libby," he called softly.

"Over here, Ike."

"Libby," he scraped one booted toe through the dust. "I-I'm sorry I swore at you."

Libby stared at him. Never before had he showed remorse for any of the outrageous things he said. "It's all right, Ike, I forgive you." She laid her hand gently on his shoulder. To her surprise he winced and jumped away. "Ike, is something wrong?"

For a moment the mask dropped from Ishmael's face. "The good pastor heard what I said last night and told my foster father."

"And he beat you."

"It doesn't matter." Ishmael pulled himself erect painfully. "I'll do it again when I feel like it. But never at you, Libby. I promise." He turned and melted into the bushes.

Libby spent most of the day alone cleaning house while Mistress Rowlandson and the girls helped Mistress Kerley, Ishmael's foster mother, with a quilt. With each task she found herself praying for Ishmael. It was his day to herd the village cattle. Perhaps in the solitude of the nearby hills he could find some peace.

When the Rowlandsons returned, Mary provided the finishing touch to a miserable day. "Ishmael's in the pillory! Serves him right for swearing at you," she said.

Libby's hand clenched over the wooden trencher she was carrying to the table board. Couldn't they see what they did to Ishmael? Each harsh punishment—each time they labeled him hopeless, rebellious, or sinner—they pushed him farther from the truth, farther from everything they wanted him to be, or that God had intended him to be.

Suddenly the house, the entire village stifled her! Snatching a cup she dashed outside. By the time she reached the well, Libby's tears flowed. Hastily she filled the cup with cold water. No matter what happened, she had to see Ishmael.

By the time she reached the village common, Libby was panting. *At least no one's seen me*, she thought. Libby hugged the houses around the square, staying beneath the second-story overhangs until she came directly behind the pillory. Taking one last look, she dashed across the open space, crouching behind Ishmael. "Ike." He did not respond.

"It's me, Libby. I didn't know 'til now. Are you thirsty?"

She heard steps behind her. Quickly Libby slipped in front of the pillory and ducked out of sight. She extended the cup carefully. Ishmael drained it in a single gulp.

Filth plastered his face. Blood streaked across his mouth and an ugly welt rose on his forehead. "It isn't fair!" Libby said. "You were sorry."

"You don't think I'd tell *them!*"

"Did they give you a chance?" Libby burst into tears.

"Libby! Don't!" Ishmael's voice cracked. "I can't stand it! I can take anything they want to do to me. But don't you cry."

Libby scooted to one side so the passer-by couldn't see her. Obediently she squelched her tears and dashed across the common, up the path, and into the Rowlandson necessary house. Only in the outdoor toilet could she expect privacy.

It was there Mistress Rowlandson found her. "What's the matter, child?" The concern in her voice renewed Libby's tears. What right had she to kindness when Ishmael had no one?

"I-I'm not feeling well," she said honestly.

"My sisters can care for the girls. Young Joseph knows how to cook for himself and his father," Mistress Rowlandson continued briskly. "Lunch isn't ready, but there are corn bread and milk. We can leave in an hour." She turned to John. "Can you start back then?"

John shrugged his shoulders. "Not unless I can exchange my horse for a fresh one. I'll be through Lancaster again in a couple of weeks with Daniel Gookin."

"I'm sure my husband or one of my brothers-in-law can arrange that," Mistress Rowlandson said.

Libby stared at her. "You mean you are going, too?"

"It would never do for you to travel alone."

Both Libby and Mrs. Rowlandson ran toward the house. Mistress Rowlandson took charge. "Libby, stir the fire and put on water for dish washing. Mary, pack clothing for yourself and Sarah. Sarah, run to your Aunt Divoll's and tell her what has happened. Mary will come later. You two will stay there until Libby and I get back."

"Yes, Mama."

"Libby, while the water heats, pack what you need." Libby rolled a change of clothing and her Bible into a blanket, then scrambled down the ladder to wash the breakfast dishes.

"You must be tired and hungry," she said to John.

"I am. I rode all night."

Swiftly Libby filled a trencher with cold porridge, and poured milk for him to drink. "Do you want tea? The water is almost hot."

"Yes, thank you." John bent his head over the filled trencher. Before she finished the other dishes, he handed it to her. "Now I should survive another day's riding."

"You must be exhausted. Maybe we should wait longer," Libby said.

"We don't dare! I'll make it."

A cold lump settled in Libby's stomach. She stuffed the last dish into its place, while Mistress Rowlandson wrote housekeeping instructions for her husband and young Joseph.

John carried their bundles to the yard. "It's a long way to the nearest inn," he reminded them. "You'd best grab a bite, too."

Libby mixed butter and molasses and spread it on slices of bread for each of them. Mistress Rowlandson poured tea.

In spite of the tea, Libby's lunch stuck in her throat. *Please, God, don't let anything happen to Father!*

Pastor Rowlandson prayed with them before they mounted. "Commit yourself to God's will, Libby," he admonished.

"I shall," she promised quietly. But could she? When she read her Bible it seemed easy to love and trust God. But the preaching at the meetinghouse made Him seem stern and far away.

She had imagined God as a loving father like her own.   But God had forgotten her, and Father lay dying. Suddenly dizzy, she clung, shaking, to the saddle.

Trees hemmed the trail on either side, cutting off the sun. Ahead of her, John and Mrs. Rowlandson vanished around a curve. Sensing her uncertainty, the horse stopped. *I should kick him,* Libby thought. But she could not persuade herself to move. "I'm alone!" She said it out loud. "No relatives nearer than England—and debts instead of money. God has changed, and no one on earth has a reason to care." But as she spoke, her panic passed. "I can't give up." She nudged the horse with her heel and it plodded on.

She found John and Mistress Rowlandson waiting for her around the bend. "Are you all right, child?" Mrs. Rowlandson asked.

Libby nodded, not trusting herself to speak.

On the narrow trail John took the lead. But when it widened he dropped back to ride beside Libby.

"Tell me about Father," she said. "Has he been sick long?"

"He coughed when he came to us," John said. "Mistress Eliot, the pastor's wife, gave him herbs to brew for his cough. He and I were sure he was recovering. But a week ago a fever struck him. He grows weaker every day."

Libby groaned. Why had she persuaded Father to come to New England? But she knew. Debtors' prison would have killed him. At least here he had a chance.

"He can't die." Libby choked on the words. "He hasn't worked his time."

"Forget the work, Libby. Just pray for your father." He paused. "I wish I were a doctor now. There must be something someone could do."

He cares, Libby thought. She gave him a shaky smile.

"Your father is a good friend," John said. "I can talk to him about things that upset my stepfather, and he understands."

Libby tried vainly to swallow the lump in her throat. "I know." The horses stopped to drink at a small stream, then plodded up a steep hill. When they reached the top John spoke again. "Your father made me these boots."

Libby surveyed the boots carefully. Yes, they looked like Father's work—fine leather, plain and sturdy with careful workmanship, but no ornament. "He must have loved making them," she said.

"He did. And they gave my stepfather the idea of having him make shoes to sell."

They passed the night in a rough cabin that served as inn and tavern where two trails crossed. Libby choked down most of a bowl of cornmeal porridge even lumpier than her first attempt. Afterward she and Mistress Rowlandson retired to a rough chamber furnished only with a limp feather bed. Libby shivered a little in the breeze that flowed unhindered through cracks in the clapboard siding.

As she crawled under the covers the cold seemed to settle in her heart. Father dying? Impossible! He had planned so eagerly for their life together after they had completed their indentures.

Yet Libby could not doubt the message. Was she not here in this beastly inn with Mistress Rowlandson tossing restlessly beside her? That very fact was proof enough.

Libby awakened to the sound of voices in the room below. *I must have slept after all,* she thought, surprised. She and Mistress Rowlandson dressed quickly, smoothed their hair as best they could, and settled their hoods in place.

After a hasty breakfast (last night's leavings, half warmed) they set off. "We should make Roxbury by noon," John said.

"That late?" Libby asked.

"If we ride hard, we could cut off an hour or so."

"Let's try."

John looked at her intently. "Are you an experienced rider?"

Libby blushed. "No. But I'll manage. I have to."

John nudged his mount to a trot. "All right. I'll hurry."

Libby followed his example. The first few strides nearly jolted her from the sidesaddle, but she clung doggedly. After a few minutes, she caught the knack of moving with the horse.

Beside her, John smiled. "Good. You do learn fast."

"Thanks." Libby's attention returned to her riding. "Hurry, hurry!" the horse's hoofs seemed to say. "Hurry! Hurry!"

They rode into Roxbury shortly before noon. John's mother met them at the door of the comfortable two-story house. "Thank goodness you're here," she said to Libby. "He's upstairs."

But before they could reach the top step, another woman appeared at the head of the stairs. One glance at her tired face told Libby the truth: They were too late.

"You must be Libby," the woman said. "I'm Hannah Eliot." Numbly, Libby followed Mistress Eliot into the room. Father's form shaped the blankets on the bed. His brown hair fell over one eye as it always did. But he was not there. She braced herself against the straight backed chair by the bedside. No Father! Never had she imagined a world without Father. Now she must live in it.

She felt John's hand grip her shoulder. "I'm sorry, Libby." His hoarseness matched the lump in her throat. She turned to face him. Seeing the tears in his eyes released hers to flow.

"Let me help with the laying out," Mistress Rowlandson said. "It's the least I can do." Libby stood frozen, staring at the familiar form that was no longer Father.

Finally Mistress Eliot noticed her. "Don't brood, child. Mistress Bassett needs thy help in the kitchen." In the kitchen, Libby's hands worked efficiently, shaping biscuits and stirring beans. Libby stared at them, surprised. Inside she felt frozen, unable to think or feel.

John's voice recalled her to the real world. "Come out with me, Libby," he said. "The air will do you good."

"Go with him, I can finish." Mrs. Bassett said.

Libby settled her hood in place, fastened her shawl, and allowed John to lead her to the street. "Walk, Libby. Don't try to think. Give God a chance to meet you."

Libby quickened her stride, wondering if she could outpace the tears John's words had roused. "I don't want Him."

"Libby!"

She whirled to face him. "Go ahead. Preach. I won't listen."

John laid a hand on each shoulder. "Don't, Libby! Don't rebel! I know it's hard. I lost my father when I was six. But we can't blame God."

"I could!" Libby gasped at her own words. "I don't mean it! I don't!"

She wanted to cry—to scream. But she could force nothing past the dry burning in her throat. Suddenly her circling thoughts burst from their channel. "What if Father had no witness of salvation? What if-if he was damned?"

For a long time John didn't answer. Overhead, birds sang. She fumbled for a rock or clod—anything to stop their spontaneous joy. She found nothing.

Libby swallowed fast, trying to wash away the stubborn burning. It didn't budge. Still silent, John took her hand and led her through an alley to a deserted garden.

"Libby, just trust. Your father did. We have to leave him in God's hands." John sounded dogmatic like Mr. Rowlandson, and unsure at the same time.

"Don't preach!"

John straightened his shoulders. "We can't know, Libby, but no man untouched by God could live as your father did."

His words slashed away the last of Libby's self control. "But what will I do now?" She buried her head in the folds of his shirt.

"You have friends, Libby. You're not alone." John handed her his handkerchief and stood patting her shoulder awkwardly.

The sun hung low on the western horizon when she returned it to him, sodden.

"Let me show you the town," John said. "I suppose it's not much compared to London. But it's comfortable, and convenient to Boston."

"London was miserable." Libby said. "The whole city burned when I was a baby. And the year before that plague killed my older brothers. People starve there today! We always ate, but I had nightmares about debtors' prison. They'd have come true, too, if we hadn't left." She shuddered. "But we had a good life. If you could see the little pickpockets! Scarcely a rag to their bones in winter. They risk hanging every day. But they have to steal or starve. Don't worry, I'll like Roxbury."

"There's stealing here, too." John said soberly. "And drunkenness. But no excuse. There's work for everyone."

They passed the meetinghouse—larger than the one at Lancaster, but equally plain. As they approached the other side of the square Libby saw the pillory. A girl about her own age stood in it with her head and hands secured. Half dried egg plastered her forehead and a fresh bruise blotched one cheek. Instinctively Libby turned her head.

"Pay her no mind," John said. "'Tis Betsy Talmadge, an indentured servant. A troublemaker."

"What did she do?"

"Stole a cup of her master's whiskey for her beau."

Libby shuddered. It was a stupid thing to do, she knew. But she couldn't help asking, "How long has she been there?"

"All day. She's quite accustomed to it, I believe."

"Couldn't they do something else?"

"Better this than lose her soul," John said grimly.

"But will it help? If they did that to Ishmael, he'd declare war on God forever."

"What punishment would you choose?"

Libby didn't answer. Taking her pocket handkerchief, she moistened it in a little puddle, and walked up to the girl. The girl stared at Libby angrily.

"Let me clean your face," Libby said softly. "I'm sure it will feel better." As she approached, Libby nearly gagged. The egg was rotten.

The girl stared silently, but Libby could feel her shivering. Quickly she untied her own shawl and laid it across the girl's shoulders. "They'll release you after sundown. Leave the shawl on the kitchen doorstep at Zedekiah Bassett's. I'll find it."

"You'll never see it again." John said.

"You might be surprised."

"I hope I'm wrong."

"So do I," Libby said. "But you don't fight anger with cruelty. I learned that from Ishmael."

They turned back to the Bassett house. When Libby glanced at John his eyes no longer smiled back. He seemed lost in unhappy thoughts. *What happened?* Libby wondered. *Is he angry about Betsy or is it because I mentioned Ishmael? I'll never understand boys.*

At the house John led her through a back entrance. Libby scrambled up the stairs before anyone could see her, and removed her hood. *I hope I get the shawl back before Mistress Rowlandson notices. She'd never understand.*

Libby rose early the next morning and hurried downstairs. When she opened the kitchen door, she saw only the doorstep, frost coated under the morning fog. *Now what do I do?* she thought. *I have to have a shawl! What will Mistress Rowlandson say?* Shivering a little she peeked under the bushes beside the door. Nothing!

Then a footstep crunched on the frozen ground and Betsy emerged from behind a rosebush. She extended the shawl silently.

"I hope it helped," Libby said. "John says you're used to the pillory, but I don't believe it. Nobody could get used to that. It's too horrible." Betsy didn't answer. Libby asked impatiently, "Can't you talk,"

"Y-y-y-y-es, M-m-ma'am."

"Thank you for bringing the shawl. I really need it."

"I-I d-d-didn't want t-to."

"But you did, Betsy," Libby said. "I knew you would. I wish I lived here instead of Lancaster. I'd like to see you again."

Betsy stared blankly.

She can't believe me, Libby realized.

Then the girl's eyes filled with tears. "Me too," she said. And this time she did not stutter.

They held Father's funeral in early afternoon. Afterward a small group gathered in the church yard for the last prayer before burial. The sun had burned away the fog, and the honey scent of springtime filled the air. Heaven must smell like this. Tears blurred Libby's eyes. *Father is happy*, she thought. *Surely he's with Jesus.* Then the grave diggers began throwing dirt over the lowered casket. Libby turned and fled.

Through the blur of tears she saw two children playing in the street. They laughed and whooped with an abandon she had not heard in the New World. Listening, she felt the tightness in her throat loosen. A small boy flew by her, with his brother racing behind him. Following them came an Indian man. He laughed, too, and called to the children.

An Indian family! she thought, envying their closeness. *What makes Puritan parents so strict?* She could not imagine Mr. Rowlandson indulging his children as the Indian did. Even her father and mother had expected her to take life seriously. Nor did they talk about love. *But I knew*, Libby thought.

In spite of her sadness, a smile played about her lips. *My parents left me good memories.* No matter what happened to her now, she would face it and make them proud. By the time she reached the Bassett home Libby could think of the future with only a faint nagging fear.

"Don't worry, Libby," Mistress Rowlandson told her that night. "Mr. Rowlandson and I are happy with your work. You may continue to work for us after your indentures are fulfilled until you marry. Or, perhaps you could conduct a Dame school. You're well fitted for the work."

"Thank you. I do my best. I-I know what I owe you. And it's more than my indentures. You've let me live in your family." *Dame school?* Libby thought. For a moment she pictured herself teaching the alphabet to a roomful of little Sarahs. *I could do that.* Then love for Mistress Rowlandson flooded her. *How God has blessed me!*

Libby thought of Betsy. *For all her anger and thieving ways, she feels alone and scared to death.*

"I'll be glad to get home," Mistress Rowlandson said, sighing. "I've never left the girls before."

"I will, too." As she said it, Libby realized that Lancaster truly had become her home. She wanted to hug Mistress Rowlandson. But the thought of Mistress Rowlandson's face if she should try such a thing, made her settle for smiling at her gratefully.

Chapter 7

War Clouds

Have you heard of anyone in town from Lancaster?" Mistress Rowlandson asked Mr. Bassett at dinner the next day. "We came in such a hurry that I forgot to ask, but I had thought my brother-in-law might be coming for supplies."

"No, I haven't. But I wouldn't recommend traveling back alone."

Mistress Rowlandson looked worried. "We must find some way home."

"You're welcome to stay here another day," Mistress Bassett said.

"I need to get back to the children."

"I'll see what I can do for you," Mr. Bassett said. "I'm going back to my office after dinner. While I'm out I'll ask around to see if I can find anyone traveling that way."

"Thank you."

"By the way," Mr. Bassett said, "had you heard of the Sassamon trial in Plymouth?"

Mistress Rowlandson nodded.

"The trial is over," Mr. Bassett continued. "They hanged three guilty Indians. But one didn't die. Afterward the poor man offered to confess." He laughed heartily. "That is he confessed that the two who died were guilty. He'll hang again. Be sure of it."

"I'm afraid there'll be Indian trouble this year," John said soberly.

"What was the Sassamon trial?" Libby asked.

"John Sassamon was a Christian Indian down in Plymouth Colony," John explained. "But he had been closely connected with Philip. Last winter Sassamon reported that the Indians were planning a general uprising. No one believed him, but only a few weeks later his body was found by a pond."

"I'm afraid John's right about trouble," Mr. Bassett said. "Whether or not there was anything to Sassamon's story of a conspiracy, King Philip is angry now because authorities hanged the murderers. The Indians simply don't understand justice."

I'm not sure I do, either, Libby thought, remembering Goodman Isaac Matthews' welcome to The Bay and the rotten egg on Betsy's face.

Mr. Bassett pushed back his chair and started toward the door, reaching for his cloak as he went. But before he could settle it over his shoulders, someone knocked.

"Come in," Mr. Bassett said, opening the door.

As the guest entered, Libby recognized Daniel Gookin, John's companion on his first visit to Lancaster. "Can you spare John again, Zedekiah? I need to visit the Praying Villages as soon as possible."

"Do you think it's safe?"

"Of course it's safe." Daniel Gookin sounded exasperated. "The Praying Indians are our brothers. But Pastor Eliot and I feel we need to reassure them of our trust."

"I can't spare John. I'm short-handed right now."

"But . . ." John began.

"No, John," Mr. Bassett said firmly. "It's entirely too risky."

"Then let me escort Mistress Rowlandson back to Lancaster." John said.

Mr. Bassett shook his head.

"Perhaps I could be of some help," Daniel Gookin said. "If I begin my tour with the New Villages, I can pass through Lancaster on my way."

Mistress Rowlandson smiled. "I should be most grateful." When they left at daybreak they found a generous lunch in a basket at the foot of the stairs. John waited outside, holding their horses.

"I'll miss you," he told Libby. "May I come to Lancaster when I get the chance?"

"Oh, yes."

"He's a fine young man," Mistress Rowlandson said as the house vanished behind them in the morning mist.

"He is, indeed." Daniel Gookin agreed. "He's been a true friend to the Praying Indians. If there is to be Indian trouble, they will need friends like him. If it ever came to open war, I fear for their safety."

"If it came to war, the farther I lived from their villages, the safer I would feel," Mistress Rowlandson said.

When they reached the end of the rutty Roxbury street, they had to go single file. As they moved away from The Bay and rivers, the mist vanished. But overhanging trees soon filtered the sunlight.

Libby's horse splashed its way along the mucky trail. She looped her skirts higher. Had only three months passed since her first trip to Lancaster? London and the ship felt a lifetime away. She could hardly wait now, to get home.

Will there be Indian trouble, she wondered. She thought of the fur-trading Indian who had frightened Sarah when they visited the Kerleys. Twice since she had seen Indians in Lancaster—shy, but proud men and women who came to trade. She began to list questions in her mind for Daniel Gookin.

At noon Daniel Gookin led them into a little clearing just off the trail. At one side a late-blooming dogwood carpeted the grass with white. Azaleas splashed color against the brushy walls. Libby slid off her horse gratefully, and settled herself in a sunny spot. Mistress Rowlandson uncovered the basket and distributed corncakes and chicken.

After a few bites Libby began her questioning. "Who is King Philip?" she asked. "Last night I heard Mr. Bassett say he is angry."

"King Philip is the English name for Metacomet, sachem or chief of the Wampanoags," Daniel Gookin explained. "You may have heard of his father, Massassoit, who befriended the early colonists at Plymouth. Philip was generally friendly until his brother, Alexander, died of a fever in a white man's home. Some Indians think whites poisoned him. Philip has hunted excuses to make trouble ever since. Now he's found one."

"I see," Libby said thoughtfully.

"I'm not quite sure what to think," Daniel Gookin continued. "At one time John Sassamon was Philip's personal scribe, so his warning may have been accurate."

"Scribe?" Libby asked.

"Yes. Several of the sachems employ them to handle correspondence with white men."

Libby frowned. "But I thought the Indians were savages."

"They had no writing until John Eliot invented an alphabet for them, but they learn fast, Daniel Gookin said. "We have had a number of Praying Indians at Harvard. One graduated."

"But they remain primitive," Mistress Rowlandson said.

"Not all." Daniel Gookin's voice rose as he warmed to his favorite subject. "They love their Bibles as much as any of us. Printer James rejoices in the fact that he set type for his people's Bible."

"But why are the Indians angry?" Libby asked. "I mean why besides the fact that we hung the murderers?"

Daniel Gookin looked thoughtful. "I've heard several grievances. At least one is justified."

"What's that?" Mistress Rowlandson demanded.

"Some of the more enlightened sachems complain about whiskey. Until white settlers came, they knew neither liquor or drunkenness. Now it is a curse."

"But Ishmael told me it's illegal to sell them liquor," Libby said.

"True. But many traders ignore the law. Usually no one prosecutes."

"I agree something should be done," Mistress Rowlandson said. "But can't they discipline their drunken as we do?"

Daniel Gookin sighed. "Indians simply don't think as civilized men do. The burden of responsibility lies on us." He pulled himself to his feet. "Time to go."

"What else angers them?" Libby asked.

Daniel Gookin smiled. "Cows in their cornfields. They simply can't see that the logical thing to do with a field is to fence it as we do. Instead they tell us to control our livestock."

Libby boosted herself into the saddle. "They were here first."

"So they were." Smiling, Daniel Gookin nodded agreement. They rode silently except for where the trail widened, allowing Mistress Rowlandson and Daniel Gookin to ride abreast. Alone behind them Libby's thoughts shuttled between John's promise to visit, and Sarah and Mary waiting for them at home.

When they reached Lancaster the next day they stopped first at Mistress Rowlandson's sister's home for Mary and Sarah. Mary walked soberly beside Libby's horse. "Is your father better?" she asked.

Libby shook her head. "We-we buried him two days ago. I didn't even get to see him alive." The tears she had forgotten all day settled in her throat and eyes.

"I'm sorry," Mary said. "Don't cry, Libby. You can be my big sister if you like."

Libby swallowed hard, forcing her words across the barrier in her throat. "Thank you, Mary. I'd like that a lot."

They had scarcely reached the dooryard when Ishmael appeared carrying a bucket. "Your sister sent you stew for supper," Mistress Rowlandson. He turned to catch Libby as she slid down.

"Thanks Ike. It's good to be home"

"It's no fun reading when you're not around, Libby."

"I guess I'm here forever, now." Her voice broke.

"You mean your father . . .? "

"Yes." She straightened her shoulders. "But Mistress Rowlandson says I can stay here and work until I marry."

"That won't be long if I have my way."

Libby glared at him. "How can you say such a thing at a time like this?"

Ishmael grinned. "So I forgot propriety again! I'll wait until next year and say it if that will make you feel any better."

In spite of herself, Libby smiled. "You can't do anything for four years. By then you may not want to." Thank God Ishmael and John did not live in the same town. They both acted like they owned her!

That night at dinner Daniel Gookin told Mr. Rowlandson about the hangings in Plymouth. "We're at the edge of trouble, I'm afraid," he concluded.

"Perhaps so. But Lancaster is a long way from Plymouth and the Wampanoags," Mr. Rowlandson said.

"If John Sassamon's warning was true, there could be a general uprising. If not, I'd still look for local trouble from Philip."

Mr. Rowlandson looked thoughtful. "We'll try to stay in close contact with The Bay."

By Sunday, life had resumed its normal routine. As usual Ishmael walked her home after the afternoon meeting. And as usual, Pastor Rowlandson watched their every move. Libby knew that he disapproved, but Mistress Rowlandson had told him pointedly how Ishmael's attitude had improved, and that she and her sister appreciated Libby's influence on him. Ishmael was her foster nephew. There was little Pastor Rowlandson could say.

That evening for the first time Ishmael took his turn as they read. "I knew you could do it!" Libby said as he returned the book to her. "I'm proud." Ishmael blushed.

"So he can read?" Mr. Rowlandson said when Ishmael had gone. "I knew he was stubborn, but he nearly convinced me he was unteachable."

"He thought so, too," Libby said. "Maybe that's why he'd quit trying."

"Don't let him fool you, Libby. There's bad blood there. And it's obvious he's interested in you. Now that you've made your point the lessons must stop."

The following week Mr. Rowlandson went to The Bay. He returned with encouraging news. "John Easton, deputy governor of Rhode Island, is leading a delegation to meet with Philip. He hopes to mediate the dispute. Lord willing we'll escape trouble yet." He paused. "Only a Quaker would try to pacify them! But I suppose I should be grateful."

Libby breathed a sigh of relief. She knew that the Rowlandsons distrusted the Indians, but they seemed unafraid. Only Sarah regarded Indians with almost hysterical fear.

June went out with grey skies and spitting rain. Men and boys worked long hours loading clumsy carts and rakes, loading and hauling their hay to safety.

One day at noon clouds overhead threatened thunder at any time. "Libby, we need you in the field this afternoon," Mr. Rowlandson told her, gulping a cup of milk. "Dinner can wait."

In the field Libby handled the unwieldy pitchfork cautiously, watching the others.

"Not like that," Ishmael told her impatiently. "We can't be here all day."

"Show me, then."

"Like this." Ishmael demonstrated.

Libby took a new grip. She could load the pitch-fork much fuller, but she still managed to drop at least half each load. She could feel Ishmael's eyes watching her disapprovingly. *It isn't fair. I never yelled at him about reading*, she thought.

The last cart load reached the barn just as the rain broke. "You may go now, Libby," Mr. Rowland-son told her.

She stopped at the back step to wash her face in the basin Mistress Rowlandson had set out for the workers, and removed her cap long enough to smooth her hair. Inside she sank wearily onto the settle. Broken blisters burned her hands.

Sarah brought her a dish of porridge and a piece of salted cod. "Mama says you should eat before you take over the ironing."

Libby groaned. She didn't know if she could stand up another minute. But when she finished her late lunch she took a flatiron and went to work. She couldn't help envying Mary whose task was turning the supper roast on the spit.

Mr. Rowlandson had barely started prayers that evening when someone banged on the door. Mr. Kerley, Ishmael's foster father, burst in, followed by his son, Ransomed, and Ishmael. "It's finally started!" he announced. "Savages looted and burned in Swansea on the twentieth. There have been several pitched battles since."

"Oh, no!" Mistress Rowlandson exclaimed.

The world seemed to fall away from Libby, leaving her dangling precariously in midair. *This can't be happening*! she thought. *It isn't real*.

Little Sarah began to cry. Libby pulled the child to her lap. "Don't be afraid," she whispered. "Swan-sea's a long way from here. We'll all take care of you."

Mistress Rowlandson took Sarah from Libby and sat rocking her. But Sarah continued to sob. "I'm scared, Mama."

"They're trying to raise militia at The Bay," Mr. Kerley said. "They'll get few from Lancaster, though."

"You mean they'd ask?" Mr. Rowlandson sounded surprised. "As isolated as we are, it would be suicide to send any man. They should send *us* protection."

July brought more reports of fighting near Swansea. One Monday in August Libby tackled the laundry alone. She scrubbed silently, ears tuned for any unusual sound. *Much good it will do*, she thought. *Indians make about as much noise as Ishmael when they move.* She scarcely noticed the familiar sound of clip-clopping hoofs until they stopped in the yard. "Libby?"

The half wrung breeches in her hand splashed into the tub, as she jumped toward the safety of the house.

"Relax, Libby. Indians don't call your name." She recognized John's laughing voice.

"It could have been a war whoop." She echoed his laughter. He dismounted, and together they carried water to the horse. "What brings you here?" she asked, returning to her washing.

John leaned against a nearby tree. "News. For most of the summer the militia has kept Philip and his men bottled up on Mount Hope Peninsula near Plymouth, where none of the other bands could join him. But last week they slipped across The Bay in canoes. There'll be real trouble, now."

Libby shivered. "I've never lived in the wilderness before. We could all be killed and nobody would know it for days."

"That's why I'm joining the militia," he told Libby. "Something has to be done to make the colonies safe for Christians."

"I suppose so," she agreed. "But why can't you make peace? I thought the governor of Rhode Island wanted mediation." Once again she could feel the world falling away beneath her feet. "Isn't there room for everybody?"

John shook his head. "Governor Winslow of Plymouth sent letters to Philip and to Weetamoo back in June, but it didn't do any good."

"Weetamoo?" Libby asked.

"The squaw sachem of the Pocassets," John explained.

"Daniel Gookin told me their grievances," Libby said. "They're only fighting for what they believe are their rights. Is that so different from what Cromwell did for the Puritans in England?"

John hesitated. "There's always a right side Libby. Now, as then, we're on it. And we have been fair. We've paid for all the land we took. We've no choice except fighting."

Yes, they are fair, Libby thought, *they are fair with Ishmael, too. But they taught him to hate.* "Are you sure fighting's worth it?" Libby asked. "Cromwell won, but what did he gain? Eventually even our people wanted King Charles back."

"If we don't fight we'll be burned in our beds, Libby." John shifted position. "Sometimes my heart says there should be another way, but can I trust what is 'desperately wicked and born to trouble as the sparks fly upward'?"

"But we have the mind of Christ," Libby quoted back at him.

"Libby Kendall!" John couldn't hide his shock. "That is sheer presumption! They're heathen. How do we know God didn't open this land to us because they were not worthy? I've heard more than one preacher say so."

"I thought you were a friend of the Indians."

"Praying Indians," John corrected her. "There's a world of difference."

For a long time Libby didn't answer. John had said openly what all Lancaster thought. Perhaps she *was* presumptuous. But study and pray as she might, she could find nothing to erase her feeling that something was wrong. Had the colonists turned the Indians against them in the same way the people of Lancaster had taught Ishmael to hate?

Later that evening every man and boy in Lancaster crowded into the meetinghouse to hear John's news and his plea for volunteers. But no one responded.

"It's ridiculous," Mr. Rowlandson said when he reached home that evening. "Of course we can't send anyone. With the Wampanoags recruiting other bands, we need every man here, with reinforcements from The Bay as soon as possible."

John, who had returned with Mr. Rowlandson and young Joseph, stood at the door turning his hat awkwardly in his hand. He looked suddenly tired and discouraged. Libby laid a hand on his shoulder.

"I'm sorry if I upset you," she said. "John—be careful. Please."

Chapter 8

Razor's Edge

Joseph," Sarah tugged at her older brother's hand. "Come outside with me. Please."

Joseph laid his Latin book in front of him on the puncheon floor and looked up. "In a few minutes. I have to finish this exercise."

"Now, please!" Little Sarah rocked from one foot to the other.

"What is it, Sarah? Can I help?" Mary asked.

Sarah shook her head. But she approached the table where Libby and Mary sat sewing by candle light. "I have to go to the necessary house."

"I'll go with you," Mary offered. "I've been putting it off."

"You couldn't scare an Indian away."

"I know," Mary admitted. "That's why *I've* been putting it off."

"Why don't we all go?" Libby asked. "Surely an Indian wouldn't bother three of us." What a liar she had become!

Unlike Sarah who still believed her father and big brother could protect her, Libby knew that nothing except God's intervention stood between them and destruction. "Lord, forgive the lie," she whispered. "I can't scare a baby."

"I'll go first," Libby said as they reached the path. "Sarah, give me your hand. Mary take her other hand." In her right hand Libby held a candle. Her left hand stretched behind her to Sarah as they walked single file.

No sound disturbed the warm stillness of the September night. But Libby did not take comfort in the silence. By now everyone in Massachusetts Bay Colony knew the truth: Indians did not advance; they skulked. Cattle and crops disappeared, houses burned, and men died—before anyone saw a single Indian. Small wonder Sarah refused to venture from the house alone even in daylight! Their business finished, the girls fled down the steep path.

Where were the Indians? Libby wondered. *And what happened to John?* Just yesterday she had heard of defeat at Squakeag. Indians had killed half the colonist's force. None of the survivors had seen John, the messenger told them. But neither had they found his body. "Oh Lord, let him be a prisoner, please," she whispered, then found herself wondering whether Indians tortured their captives.

The next day, corn harvest forced fear from Libby's thoughts. She and young Joseph picked the ears by hand. Then Libby joined the others shucking and hanging the ears. Mistress Rowlandson showed her how to parch what they did not dry.

Pumpkins followed corn. All one day she gathered them, and lugged them to the house. Mistress Rowlandson and Mary pealed them, and removed the seeds from the centers, cut them in small pieces, and hung them to dry.

That Sunday Mr. Rowlandson thundered a repentance sermon. "The wars are God's judgment on us," he proclaimed. "We love pleasure. Children think only of play. Women love fine clothes and gossip. God will punish! We merit His wrath. Repent!"

That night Libby awakened, shivering. She examined her own life carefully. She thought of the half lie she used each time she accompanied Sarah and Mary outside after dark. She questioned the wisdom of Pastor Rowlandson and the church. She did not oppose sin as she should. Of all these she repented heartily.

But when morning came she questioned the need. Would not God himself wish to comfort little Sarah? As for her other deviations from the path of duty, sometimes she could not reconcile Mr. Rowlandson's ideas of justice and punishment with the words of love she read in the Bible.

Libby never doubted that some sin or sins had brought punishment. But what sins were they? Libby listed her ideas in her mind: selling spirits (liquor) to the Indians, inflicting them with laws they could not understand, intolerance where the Bible taught love. Because of Ishmael she recognized each as sin. But not one item on Libby's list appeared in Pastor Rowlandson's sermons.

One Friday in late October Pastor Rowlandson called for a day of prayer and fasting. Libby fasted and prayed willingly. But as the day progressed Mary grew white and wan, and Sarah fretted. Libby found herself praying for them as much as she prayed for the colony. Could God really demand that children repent of sins they were too young to commit?

As they left the meetinghouse in midafternoon, Ishmael fell in step beside her. Since Mr. Rowlandson had stopped their reading lessons, she had seen little of him. "Hello Libby."

Libby jumped. "Ike! I didn't see you at the meetinghouse."

Ishmael grinned. "I wasn't there. I was scouting."

"I'm glad. You know the woods better than any man in the village."

"I know." Ishmael scowled. "It comes of bad blood."

"Not bad," Libby said. "Just different."

"They're one and the same," Ishmael said. "If it weren't for you and my foster mother, I wouldn't report it if I spotted a regiment of Indians."

For once he managed to shock her. "Ishmael Brown!"

"You know they treat them like dogs—" Ishmael paused, "like I treat my dog."

"Not dogs," Libby said. "More like children."

"You're right. They push children around, too."

Libby couldn't argue. Mistress Rowlandson loved her children, but she expected instant obedience and hours of work each day from Sarah and Mary. And she called them down harshly or even struck them when they deviated from her standards. On the other hand Libby's own mother had been strict. Without her training, Libby knew, she could not survive life on the frontier now.

"Maybe parents have to," she said, finally.

"Indian parents don't! I stop in Nashobah when I hunt." Ishmael paused for dramatic effect: "I have a cousin there. His father offered to take me when my real mother died. But they wouldn't let him. I wish they had."

"I didn't know there were Praying Villages near Lancaster," Libby said.

Ishmael grinned. "It's only five miles to Nashobah. I like long hunts. Mr. Kerley's given up asking where I go—as long as I don't take his son, Ransomed, with me."

"Now I am scared!" Libby smiled. "If you saw a warrior you just might offer to help."

Ishmael stopped abruptly in the path. His lips tightened into a fine line. His eyes smouldered. Never had his cheekbones seemed so high. "Don't say that, Libby Kendall! I wouldn't mind fighting *against* the whole world. But I can't fight *for* anyone because I don't belong anywhere."

"I hope you never have to choose," Libby said. "But you do belong, more than you know. Your foster mother loves you and I-I" she stopped, confused.

"You what?" Ishmael demanded fiercely.

"I-I'd hate it dreadfully if anything happened to you."

"Elizabeth!" Pastor Rowlandson stepped between them. "This is no time for dawdling. Evening chores won't wait."

"Yes, Sir." Libby scurried home. Mountains of neglected work lay waiting. But he needn't speak as though Ishmael didn't exist. No wonder Ishmael knew no loyalty except to the few who befriended him.

In the threatening silence of that night Libby confessed the sin of rebellion for the hundredth time.

Cold November days brought butchering. One night Pastor Rowlandson penned his largest pig in a stall in the barn. The next morning Libby and the men rose before dawn. She ladled out cold porridge then stirred the fire to life. When Mistress Rowlandson got up, she and the girls shared a trencher of half-warmed porridge. Then they mixed salt, water, and vinegar boiled together for pickling brine. With the brine prepared, they turned to sewing.

Outside, the men skinned and cut the meat, hanging it from tree limbs to cool. That night they feasted on fresh boiled pork, vegetables, and corn bread. Late that night Libby and Mistress Rowlandson took down the cooled pork, packed it in wood barrels, and poured the brine over it. No guilt troubled Libby's dreams that night.

In mid-November Mr. Kerley and his son, Ransomed, made a hasty trip to The Bay for supplies. When they returned, all their relatives gathered in the Rowlandson's fire room for a counsel of war.

"The Wampanoags have captured a group of Praying Indians—or so they'd have us believe," Mr. Kerley announced. "Personally, I think they defected."

"It's almost impossible to stop them," he continued. "They wipe out two thirds of a settlement before anyone sees a single Indian. By the time the militia rallies they're miles away burning another village."

"There have been heavy casualties in the militia," Ransomed added. "We begged for protection, but the governor wouldn't listen."

"We'll have to protect ourselves," Mr. Rowlandson said. "Properly fortified, we could defend our house. There's room for all of us in an emergency."

The next morning the men and boys began to erect a stockade around the house. The men sharpened poles on one end, stood them tightly together, and drove them into the ground. Once they stood in place, the boys worked with knives and hatchets sharpening the tops.

While the men worked, Libby cut a haunch from the deer Ishmael and Joseph had shot the day before, and tied a long thong to one end. Twisting it tightly, she hung it over the fire, then set tea to steeping in the largest iron pot.

Taking young Joseph's half-stitched breeches, she perched on a stool and watched the turning meat. From time to time she retwisted the string. Where was John? Dead? Captured? Had he learned to hate all Indians? Did Daniel Gookin hate the Indians now? She wondered. Did she? Should she?

Mr. Kerley took charge of construction. Libby heard him shouting orders at everyone. By dinnertime Ishmael's eyes smoldered. *He's likely to hit someone before the day's over*, Libby thought. His foster mother, Mrs. Kerley, watched him closely, too.

"Someone needs to scout," Mistress Kerley said. "Why don't we send Ishmael. He sees things no one else can."

The men agreed. Ishmael flashed his foster mother a rare smile, picked up his flintlock rifle, and sped up the trail behind the house to the forest.

By that Friday evening the Rowlandsons, Kerleys, and Divolls had completed the stockade and
prepared shooting holes for muskets in the corners
of the house. Mistress Rowlandson inspected it with
satisfaction. "It's not a real fort," she said, "but just
the same I feel less vulnerable." Libby agreed with
her.

"It's a relief to have a refuge if things get bad,"
Mistress Kerley said.

As winter deepened, Ishmael continued his daily
patrols. His face had set into a permanent mask.
No wonder most people think he has no feelings, Libby
thought. Weeks passed without word from the outside.

Then one night Ishmael bounded into the path
with a whoop as Libby climbed to the barn for the
evening milking. He lunged toward her, grabbing her
by the shoulder. Libby tried to scream, but his hand
covered her mouth.

Laughing grimly Ishmael released her.

"If you do that again, Ishmael Brown, I'll-I'll—"

"Libby, I'm sorry!" Ishmael sounded shaken. "I
wasn't thinking. I wouldn't hurt you, honest."

"What is it then?" Libby asked curtly.

"I met a Praying Indian—at least he used to
be—in the woods. He's on his way to join Canonchet,
one of the Indian leaders. They sent my uncle's
family to Deer Island in Boston Harbor—rounded up
everyone they could find in Nashobah and shipped
them off with no food! Not even their Bibles!"

"Who did that, Ishmael?"

"The bigwigs at The Bay. Libby, you've never
seen a winter around here. Deer Island's in the
harbor. They can't hunt and there's nothing to catch
but a few fish and mussels. They'll starve! How can
Christians do that to each other? Just answer me!"

"I can't, Ike. I don't know. But they keep on
doing it." She could not shut out her own memories.
"In London the King's men arrested our people and
let them rot in prison. Here in the colonies we hang

Quakers. And all of us—King's men, Puritans, or Quakers say we're Christians. Something's wrong, Ike. But I'm sure of one thing. It's us, not God."

With butchering and harvest past, Libby and Mistress Rowlandson rendered tallow for candles. Mary and Sarah, watched over by Joseph and other older boys, joined other girls "a-leafing" in the woods for the winter supply of oak leaves to lay beneath baking bread in the oven.

Christmas came without celebration. In London even Puritans couldn't escape yuletide, although they did not participate. But Massachusetts law forbade any festivity. Christmas morning everyone met in the meetinghouse—joining Puritans all over Massachusetts Bay Colony in a day of prayer and fasting. Once again Mr. Rowlandson thundered against sin. He gave special emphasis to the final one on the list. "We have tolerated Quaker meetings in our midst. Know now that those who help them or attend their devilish meetings will be fined."

But they did celebrate that month, after all. In late December several men traveled to The Bay together. They returned with good news. "We finally had a decisive victory," Mr. Divoll, Mistress Rowlandson's brother-in-law, announced. "Friendly Indians led our main forces—1,100 men—into Philip's main camp by a secret path. They set fire to everything as they came in. Hundreds of Indians died, and our men wiped out their main food supply."

Libby glanced at Ishmael. He sat staring fixedly at the wall.

One of the younger men spoke quietly. "They didn't kill warriors. They burned women and children and old people."

"An Indian is an Indian," Mr. Kerley said.

"We'll have a short service of prayer and thanksgiving at the meetinghouse tomorrow," Mr. Rowlandson announced.

No one noticed when Libby slipped out the back door. She leaned, trembling, against the railing on the porch. Children? She had seen Praying Indian children on the streets of Roxbury, laughing and playing as they followed their parents. Children like Sarah! She shuddered. "Children who never hurt anyone! They had no right," she said out loud.

She turned to see Ishmael standing next to her. "I had to come out. I thought I was going to be sick," she said.

"You really care." Ishmael sounded surprised. "Of course I do!" Libby snapped. "Don't you?"

Ishmael didn't answer. Finally Libby turned to go into the house. Just as she pulled the door shut he spoke so quietly she nearly missed his words. "I don't know, Libby. I don't know."

The Great Swamp Battle, as the men called it, didn't end Indian raids. Each time their forays devastated an isolated village Mr. Rowlandson looked more grim. Several times Ishmael reported seeing signs of Indians, or even encountering them on his patrols. Finally Mr. Rowlandson could stand it no longer. "We simply have to have militia protection," he told his wife one February evening. "I'm going to The Bay and talk to the governor. They can't ignore us out here!"

Chapter 9

Captivity

With Indians so near, everyone in Lancaster prepared for the worst. The Divolls and the Kerleys, Mistress Rowlandson's sisters and their families, brought food and clothing and livestock and then barricaded themselves inside the Rowlandson stockade. All around Lancaster other families also moved into garrison houses. No one ventured far from the stockades except Ishmael who continued his forays into the surrounding forest.

Libby envied him. Children played, studied, and squabbled in every corner. Mistress Rowlandson and her sisters argued and smoked. Older boys scuffled until their mothers banished them to the back porch to keep watch on the hill behind the house. Libby could not work or think in the confusion.

On the evening of February 9, Ishmael did not come home. Libby paced restlessly in front of the fireplace. *This can't be real,* she thought. *Tomorrow will be a day like any other. Ishmael will come in and laugh at us for being afraid.*

Mrs. Kerley smoked one pipe after another. Children clung to their mothers, too frightened to cry. No one argued that evening. They sat silent, listening and praying, waiting for what they knew must happen. The men kept watch during the night. Only the smallest children slept.

Libby rose early and peaked down the ladder hole at the men sleeping below. No Ishmael! A knot tightened itself around her stomach. She crept down the ladder and stirred the fire to life. Picking her way around and over the sleeping bodies on the floor, she stepped to the back porch where the boys had stacked firewood.

Smoke billowed from the barn. She could hear flames popping inside. The armload of wood crashed, unnoticed, at her feet.

Ducking through the door, she shrieked, "They're here!" Men yanked on breeches and ran to their stations at the shooting holes. Mothers gathered their children to them. Sarah and Mary sat motionless until Libby thrust their outer clothes at them. "Get dressed." she ordered. "Your shawls, too. We may have to run for it." They obeyed, then scrambled to their mother's side.

Libby tried to pray. Across the room she saw Mistress Divoll and Mistress Rowlandson mouthing the words of the twenty-third Psalm. Mary sniffled. Sarah clutched her mother. "Don't let go of me Mama, please."

"I won't, Baby." her mother promised.

Outside, the sun sent watery rays over the house and burning barn. If only the Indians would eat the cow and be satisfied with their damage for the day.

The rifleman posted at the back porch shouted, but rapid gunfire cut off his words. Moments later they heard flames snapping on the back porch.

Libby snatched the water bucket. Only a cupful remained. "Get the coverlets." Mrs. Rowlandson said. "We'll try to smother it."

Mr. Kerley snatched a woolen blanket from the floor and began to beat at the flames as they licked through the back door. Several other men followed his example. The women and children huddled near the front door. "Oh Lord, don't let the house burn," Libby prayed.

Then she heard what they all dreaded—flames crackling overhead. Mistress Rowlandson heard it too. She snatched Sarah to her. Only a miracle could save them now.

In minutes smoke filled the house. Flames ate quickly through the back wall and gnawed their way across the puncheon floor. Everyone crowded against the door until the unburned floor no longer held them all.

Libby coughed and shut her eyes against the stinging smoke. She had snatched her shawl, ready for the wintery outdoors and now, beneath it perspiration drenched her dress and under petticoats. As the heat intensified, Libby forgot the Indians. Only fresh, cool air mattered, now.

"We'll have to run for it." Mr. Kerley announced. "Form a line. And keep low. When we reach the yard, run zigzag and hope the savages are poor shots." He flung open the door. A volley of shots greeted the first escapees. Libby plummeted through the door, gasping. She nearly tripped over the body of one of Mistress Divoll's sons. She managed one reviving gulp of pure air before rough hands snatched at her, throwing her to the ground. Guns banged all around her. Once a bullet passed so close she could hear its whistle. Then she heard Sarah scream.

Libby squirmed into a position that let her see Mistress Rowlandson. She cradled the screaming Sarah against her, apparently ignoring the Indian who dragged them toward a horse. Blood soaked her white apron. Sarah must be badly hurt. When the Indian forced Mrs. Rowlandson to mount, she thrust Sarah at him fiercely, then snatched the child back as soon as she was seated.

Libby retched. "Oh, God, not Sarah!" she whispered. "Let it be me instead."

The Indian who had thrown Libby down prodded her with his rifle barrel, barking an order in his own language. She guessed the meaning and scrambled to her feet.

Ignoring the dead and dying, the Indians marshalled their captives and hustled them out of the stockade. Libby followed numbly along the path where she had gathered wildflowers with the girls. Ahead she could hear Sarah. Her screams had subsided to noisy sobs. Once Libby heard her ask for water.

But their captors had no mind to stop. They scrambled along the rough trail, slipping and clawing. Libby's paper-soled shoes disintegrated during the first hour of the enforced march. The stony ground gouged her feet unmercifully. But by the time the sun lightened the clouds directly above her, Libby walked on wooden feet, feeling nothing except weariness and thirst, followed by hunger. They climbed small hills and stumbled down them again. Once they crossed a frozen lake.

Late in the afternoon she discovered Mary just ahead of her. "Mary!" she called, "It's Libby. I'll try to catch up with you." Somehow she managed. Mary clung to Libby's hand until darkness fell and their captors finally stopped. They built a fire, but no one offered them food. The Indians did not eat, either, Libby noticed. She and Mary snuggled close for warmth. Mary slept, but questions raced through Libby's mind, keeping her awake. Did Ishmael lie dead in the forest like the little Divoll boy? Could they reach Mistress Rowlandson tomorrow? What about Sarah's wound? Would it heal?

The next morning they pushed on. Libby and Mary could not get near Mistress Rowlandson. But Libby saw her walking ahead of them, carrying Sarah. Sarah no longer cried. She flopped weakly over her mother's shoulder. Anger began to heat the rock that had settled in Libby's heart. Why Sarah, the little sister she had always wanted? "Please, God, don't let her die."

"I know where we are," Mary said when they made camp that night. "We're near Princeton."

This time they slept in crude lodges. By midnight the fire in the center of the crude lodge burned lower and lower. Libby sat rigidly in her place near the door. Beside her Mary curled into a tight little ball, pushing her back snugly against Libby for warmth. Only an occasional snore from a sleeping squaw broke the silence of the night. Libby thought again of Ishmael. Perhaps some other band of Indians held him captive. Would she see him—or John again? Her thoughts turned to a more practical matter. Could she slip out and find Mistress Rowlandson without being missed?

Mary fidgeted in her sleep, whimpered, then sat up, snatching Libby's arm. "What is it?" Libby asked.

"I want to see Mama," Mary quavered. "Oh, Libby what if something dreadful happens to her and Sarah! I've got to find them."

"You can't." Libby whispered. "The Indians might hurt you like they hurt Sarah. Then what would I tell your Mother?"

Mary clung to her, shaking silently. "I know." Libby stroked her hair. "I'm scared, too. But we're not licked yet. Your mother trusts me to take care of you. And I'm going to. I promise."

Gradually Mary's shaking stopped. "Can you stay alone for a while?" Libby asked softly.

Mary's hand tightened on Libby's arm. "Where are you going?"

"To see if I can find your mother and Sarah."

"What if you get caught?"

"I won't." Libby took a deep breath. "I think I know which end of the camp she's in."

"Let me go, too."

"It's too dangerous. You don't know where to look. I do, and besides that, I'm stronger."

"All right." For a moment Mary clung to Libby. "Hurry back, please! I couldn't stand it alone."

Snow swirled silently around the huddled lodges. She could see guards around the outside edges of the camp. A stick crackled under her feet and one guard turned around, but when he saw that she did not try to leave, he ignored her. Cautiously, Libby groped her way to the farthest lodge. Pulling back the door curtain, she peeped inside. Mrs. Rowlandson sat silhouetted in the light from the dying fire.

Libby held her breath as she set one cautious foot in front of the other. After what seemed like hours she reached the fire. Even then Mrs. Rowlandson did not look up. She rocked back and forth, clutching Sarah to her. A sob caught in Libby's throat. *Sarah is dead. I know it.*

"I'm sorry," Libby whispered softly.

Slowly Mrs. Rowlandson raised her head. "Oh, Libby! Have you seen Mary?"

At first Libby couldn't answer. Pictures of Sarah flashed before her: Sarah trying not to squirm in church—struggling to fold an oversize sheet—Sarah crying from Ishmael's teasing—snuggling close to Libby during family prayer—singing with Libby the day John came. Remembering her little brothers, Libby had rejoiced in Sarah's sturdiness. Her presence had softened the pain of Father's loss.

"I loved her, too," Libby whispered.

Mrs. Rowlandson laid her burden down gently. She took Libby's hand. "They wouldn't let me do a thing for her, Libby! At least she's not suffering. Who knows how long this will last?"

They sat silently as long as they dared before Mrs. Rowlandson repeated her question. "Where is Mary? Do you know?"

"We're together, but I was afraid to let her come."

"I'm glad you're looking after her, Libby."

They clung to each other, prolonging the contact as long as they dared. Finally Mrs. Rowlandson released Libby. "Go, child. Think of Mary. You mustn't risk being caught."

"All right." Libby crept from the lodge, groping blindly toward her own sleeping place.

Once there, she slipped inside the lodge, guiding herself by the sound of Mary's muffled sniffles. "Libby," Mary whispered.

"I'm here."

Mary flung herself against Libby. "Did you find Mother and Sarah?"

"Yes." Libby could scarcely force the words over the lump in her throat.

"Sarah's hurt bad, isn't she?"

"She-she died, Mary."

Mary's tears triggered Libby's own again. They clung to each other crying softly until they fell asleep.

Chapter 10

A Winter Plan

Morning came too soon. Libby's empty stomach growled and gurgled. Would anyone serve breakfast? No one did. They must not have any food. She knew Indians usually stored their crops for winter use. But the militia had destroyed large supplies of food in the Swamp Battle.

Libby glanced at the Indians around her. They looked gaunt. They had punctuated the night with rattling coughs. Nevertheless the man who had captured her and Mary nudged them to their feet with his rifle barrel. Libby's bruised and gashed feet throbbed as the Indian hurried the girls to a nearby lodge. Once Libby stumbled and he yanked her up impatiently.

Inside the lodge he shoved the girls toward an Indian woman. He grunted something. The woman agreed. Her eyes traveled from their feet to their heads. *Inspecting us*, Libby thought. She stared back.

The woman wore crude breeches with leather leggings covering her legs below. A fur cape slung across one shoulder protected her chest. Grease glistened on all the exposed parts of her body, and she had daubed her face with white paint. Libby could not guess what she really looked like.

After an animated discussion, the woman pulled a string of shells from around her neck and handed them to the man.

Mary shuddered. "See the wampum. She's buying us," she whispered to Libby.

So they were slaves! Libby grinned wryly. *Nothing's really changed*, she thought. *Except this might be forever.* Her grin changed to a frown. What if no one rescued them—ever?

Their new mistress pointed to herself. "Awatamoo," she said. Libby followed her example. "Libby," she said, then pointed to Mary: "Mary."

The camp dismantled rapidly. Awatamoo thrust heavy bundles at both girls. Mary balanced hers as best she could. "I'm hungry," she said.

Libby wrestled her load into a good carrying position. "So am I. Maybe now someone will feed us. We can't work if we're starved."

They set off along forest trails Libby could never have found alone. In spite of their empty stomachs, the Indians traveled rapidly. Mary, who had gone barefoot all summer, didn't seem to mind at first. But Libby moaned. In spite of the numbing cold, every rock and stick in the path stabbed painfully. She stumbled and fell. Without shoes she could go no farther.

Awatamoo spoke sharply. Libby lifted one foot for the woman to see. If they wanted to shoot her, they could. To her surprise Awatamoo produced a pair of moccasins from her pack. They were too large, but Libby tore strips from her petticoat and stuffed the ends and bottoms. Her feet still hurt, but at least she could walk. She smiled at Awatamoo. "Thank you." She shouldered her load again and scrambled to catch up with the group.

Although Mary had tougher feet, she lacked endurance. In early afternoon Libby transferred half Mary's load to her own bundle.

They camped that night near another settlement. Libby had no idea where they were. But she had heard its Indian name before: Menameset.

They ate soup that night. Libby watched, amazed and disgusted, as the women mixed old bones, pieces of leather and a few straggly plants into their pot. Who could eat that? But she and Mary forgot their squeamishness when someone offered them a cup to share. Two quick gulps and the cup was a third empty. It took all Libby's self-control to let Mary drink the rest. The Indians ate little more than their captives. *How do they live?* Libby wondered. She noticed a little girl about Sarah's age shivering by the fire. Was she sick?

The next morning Libby divided her attention between the Indian girl and Mary. Awatamoo carried the child for part of the morning, then set her on a horse, where she rode, shivering convulsively.

"I hope she falls off," Mary said fiercely.

One part of Libby wanted to say yes. But another part argued. *I know the Indians killed Sarah when she hadn't done anything wrong. But neither has this little girl. Hurting her won't bring Sarah back.* But she could not make herself answer Mary for a long time.

"No, Mary," she said at last. "It isn't her fault she is sick and hungry. She's little—like-like Sarah was. Here, let me take part of your load."

They plodded on silently. Libby could not remember carrying any burden so long. The work made her feel almost warm. She glanced at the little girl again, then at the Indians. Abruptly she set her burden down, pulled off her shawl, and fastened the awkward pack on her back again.

"What are you doing?" Mary demanded. "You can't be too warm."

"No," Libby said, looking at the Indian child, "but she's colder." She forced her tired legs to hurry. When she caught up with the little girl she tucked the shawl around her.

Mary repeated, "What are you doing, Libby?"

"What the Bible says," Libby said between clenched teeth.

"I can't return evil for evil. Anyway her mother probably saved my life when she gave me the moccasins."

Mary started to cry. "I hate them all. I can't help it when I think of Sarah."

"Sometimes I do too," Libby said honestly. "But we have to stop. It's wrong. I-I almost wish they'd shot me instead of Sarah."

Mary's tears stopped instantly. "Libby, don't! If they shot you, I'd die!" Someone shouted at them and both girls struggled to walk faster. "Libby," Mary said suddenly. "Where's Mother?"

"I don't know. I think she left our group."

"What if we never find her again?" Mary's voice quavered. "We will," Libby said. "Someone will rescue us."

Would they? If not, what would happen to them? She tried to ignore her thoughts. If only she could find Ishmael or John, she wouldn't feel so helpless! They both spoke Algonquian, the Indians' language. Libby glanced at Mary plodding ahead of her.

"One good thing happened today, Mary" she said. "Awatamoo paid for both of us. We'll stay together."

The following night they reached a settled village. When their owner led them into her lodge, they found a fire. For the first time since they had fled the burning house, Libby felt completely warm. She and Mary shared a small corn cake, but each girl received a whole cup of broth.

The next morning Awatamoo thrust a tightly-woven basket into Libby's hand and shoved her through the lodge door. Libby looked around her, confused, until she noticed an Indian girl with a similar basket. *I'll follow her,* she decided. *I'm probably supposed to do whatever she does.* The other girl went to a nearby stream. Taking a broken limb she began pounding the ice to crack it. Finding another stick, Libby pounded, too. When they had opened a hole near shore the Indian girl dipped her basket and filled it with water. Libby did the same.

As she approached the lodge someone called her name. Libby jumped, sloshing icy water on her legs and feet. She eased the basket to the ground and whirled.

A stocky Indian stood grinning at her. Then she recognized his blue eyes. "John! Where did you come from? Did they capture you at Squakeag?" She caught her breath. "Thank God you're alive."

"Barely. No one's eaten much at a time since the Swamp Fight. But it was worth it."

"Was it? From what I heard we slaughtered helpless children and old people just like savages. John, isn't there any way to stop this? We lose our homes and food. They lose theirs. We lose our families. They lose theirs. None of it makes sense."

John stared impassively. "This is war, Libby."

"Oh, John, they took Lancaster—and-and killed Sarah."

"And you want to stop this before it's properly finished? If we don't destroy them, they'll drive us back to England. That's what Philip has in mind."

"Does it matter? Nothing will bring Sarah back," she said. "I've no wish to see another child die, not even an Indian." ·

"I'm sorry, Libby." John's handclasp felt strong, comforting. "I should have escaped months ago, but I couldn't think how. With two of us, we'll figure out some way."

"Three of us. Mary's with me. I can't leave her."

Awatamoo pulled aside the mat covering the lodge door and shouted. Libby snatched the water basket and scurried inside, dousing her legs and moccasins again.

At Awatamoo's gesture, Libby added water to the already simmering broth pot. When it bubbled, Awatamoo added a single handful of cornmeal. Mistress Rowlandson used more in a single serving of porridge, Libby thought. But it was hot—and she and Mary were allowed two bowls. For a few minutes they forgot their hunger. The Indians fared no better, although Awatamoo gave her child a dry bone to gnaw afterward. When Libby finished she pulled moss from a nearby tree and padded her too-large moccasins.

After the meal Awatamoo bundled her utensils into a carrying basket, rolled skins and blankets into a pack, and thrust them at Libby and Mary. Libby bound the blankets to Mary's back with leather thongs Awatamoo gave her, and tied the heavier, more awkward basket on her own back.

Outside the lodge other Indians prepared to travel. By noon Libby no longer noticed hunger or cold. One foot down—then the other—pick up the first foot—adjust the pack—step over a fallen branch. Walking filled her whole mind. She had forgotten any other work—any other world.

Once Libby saw John ahead of her on the trail. For a moment she allowed herself to think of escaping with him and finding her way back to The Bay. She glanced at Mary trudging just ahead. *She'll hold out as long as we will,* Libby thought. *We could make it.* One foot struck a large rock imbedded in the path. Libby caught her balance forgetting everything except her plodding feet.

That night they reached another settled camp. Except for hunger Libby and Mary rested comfortably on the sleeping shelf along the lodge wall. Once Libby awakened to the sound of coughing around her. *Half of them are sick,* Libby thought. *And no wonder. They've lost their homes and their food supplies. We all have, and nobody has gained anything.*

Awatamoo woke Libby early the next morning and thrust the water basket into her hands. Without her paint, Awatamoo looked almost friendly, Libby thought.

When she returned with water, Libby could see that Awatamoo's little girl, Weetashonks, was feverish. Awatamoo busied herself brewing some kind of herb drink for the child. In an hour the child seemed better. *Whatever is in it must work*, Libby thought. *I wonder if John knows what they use.*

After they had drunk their watery gruel, Awatamoo brought out a length of linsey woolsey and indicated to Libby and Mary that she wanted a dress like theirs.

Libby spread the fabric on the floor, trying to estimate how many yards in it. *Who wove it, and what happened to her?* Libby asked herself. *I can't believe Awatamoo bought it.* "The skirt will be easy," she said to Mary. We can get a long leather strip and tie a knot in it for her waist measurement and another for the skirt length.

"What about the bodice?" Mary asked.

"We'll cross that bridge when we come to it, but we can measure the same way, I think."

By the time darkness fell Libby had marked the fabric and cut the pieces with a pair of scissors that Awatamoo loaned her reluctantly. *More loot from some colonist*, Libby decided.

Awatamoo thought of everything, even thread. "Mary, you can start a straight seam for the skirt," Libby said. While Mary worked, Libby studied the scraps carefully. The piece was a neutral color. Evidently no one had had time to dye it.

Working quickly, Libby folded a large scrap and cut two rough human shapes, then stitched the pieces together. She pulled dry grass from the ground in one corner of the lodge to stuff the crude doll.

"What are you doing?" Mary asked.

"Making a poppet for Weetashonks. But I need something for a face."

"Your shawl is raveling," Mary said. "You could pull a little red yarn for a mouth."

"Good. I'll break a couple of buttons off my underpetticoat. That'll make eyes."

Awatamoo smiled when she saw the finished doll, and handed Libby leather scraps to dress it.

"Oooh," Weetashonks squealed when Libby gave it to her. Libby smiled. "All children sound the same when they're happy," she told Mary. "I'll start the other skirt seam now."

By the time she and Mary found places on the sleeping shelf that night, Weetashonks slept soundly, holding her poppet doll close. Libby curled against Mary for warmth. Making the doll had loosened the knot of fear and anger that usually tightened at night. Sleep came quickly.

The next morning when Libby went for water she saw John upstream. He walked onto the ice, then stamped, as though to test it. Nodding as though satisfied, he joined Libby.

"What were you doing?" she asked.

"If we get away, we have to do it while everything is frozen. Otherwise they'll track us. The best thing we could do would be walk down the middle of a frozen stream."

"How much longer will the freeze hold?"

"What month is it?" John asked. "March?"

"Probably late February. They burned Lancaster February 10."

"We probably have another two weeks. Our only problem is knowing where to go."

"You've traveled all over this country with Daniel Gookin," Libby said. "You must know where we are."

"I do," John said. "But I don't know which settlements have been evacuated or destroyed. There's no food here to steal, so we can't travel far. Meantime I'm working on some kind of weapons. We'll never manage a gun. But if we can get a knife, fish line, and hooks, we might manage for several days."

Libby glanced at her basket guiltily. "I have to get back or Awatamoo will be angry."

"You're lucky she's in charge of you," John told her. "She's kinder than most of them."

"I almost like her," Libby admitted. "It's good to be around little Weetashonks. It keeps me from missing Sarah so much."

For the next week Libby and Mary spent hours each day sewing. Awatamoo provided everything they needed. At the appropriate time she even brought out buttons.

When they finished, Awatamoo donned her English outfit immediately, then daubed fresh paint on her face. "She's ruining it!" Mary whispered. "Why dress like a white man and wear Indian paint?"

"It does spoil the effect!" To hide her laughter, Libby turned to the sleeping shelf, pretending she had lost something. Mary hurried to help her.

A moment later Awatamoo beckoned the girls to follow her. Slowly they all paraded through neighboring lodges, showing off her finery. Every time Libby caught sight of Awatamoo's painted face, she choked off another wave of giggles.

"Thank God you were here, Libby," Mary said when they curled on the sleeping shelf that night. "I can sew seams and make buttonholes. But I could never fit a bodice or cut one out."

Libby smiled. "You did your share. We're a good team. Maybe we can go in business when we get back." Mary laughed.

During the week of sewing Libby saw John only once. But the morning after she finished, John beckoned to her as she dipped water. Looking around to make sure no one noticed, she put down the basket and followed him to a nearby thicket. He lifted a flat rock and pulled a knife and coil of twine out of the depression below. "I've got most of what we need. When we travel again, we'll find our chance. And then—" Loud voices nearly drowned out the last words. Libby looked up to find a group of Indian men glaring at them ominously. And with them she saw—Ishmael.

Chapter 11

Coals of Fire

One of the men barked a question. John hesitated, then answered in Algonquian.

Someone slammed Libby to the ground, driving her into a sharp rock. Again and again her attacker bludgeoned her. Libby screamed once. But her next breath triggered stabbing pain, stifling her cry. She tried to roll away, but a scowling Indian pushed her back. By the time her tormenters gave up their sport, she knew nothing.

Libby awoke with the vague feeling that something was wrong. Unconsciously she tensed herself, waiting for the next blow. Nothing happened. From somewhere nearby she heard low moaning. Turning her head, the only part of her body that did not ache unbearably, she saw John sprawled a few feet away.

"What happened?" she asked.

John swore—softly at first, then louder.

Libby gasped. "Don't! That hurts as much as everything else." She tried to pull herself to a sitting position, but every movement sent stabbing pains through her back and ribs. Stifling a groan, she slumped to the ground again.

John didn't move. "Your fine friend Ishmael betrayed us! He saw me at the cache earlier and told the warriors."

Ishmael! A traitor? Libby gagged at the thought, then spat blood. Her tongue throbbed where her teeth had gashed when she fell. She had laughed at Ishmael when he told her he had bad blood. And foolishly, she had trusted his loyalty.

"I'll kill him!" John said, rolling toward a nearby tree. He grasped a branch and pulled himself to his feet. For a long time he stood panting, propped against the tree. "I'll kill him," he repeated when he could speak.

I should stop him, Libby thought. *But he might as well. Nobody would care.* She tried again to raise herself, then began crawling toward the lodge. She had nowhere else.

Awatamoo ignored her, when at last she reached the lodge and hoisted herself onto the sleeping platform. But Mary brought a leather robe and covered her. "Libby! What happened?"

Libby's heart pounded. Perspiration dribbled across her face, and her clothes felt clammy against her. She couldn't answer.

Mary began to cry. "Libby, don't die. Please."

"I've no intention of dying," she managed to whisper. But each breath tortured her battered ribs. "They found out we were trying to escape."

"Escape?" Mary sounded shocked.

"Not without you," Libby reassured her. "But we were planning. I didn't want to tell you until everything was ready." She shut her eyes.

Libby slept restlessly, aware even in sleep that she must not move. After a few hours little Weetashonks crawled in beside her and lay, coughing. The child's warmth comforted her. Gradually her body subsided to a dull ache and Libby could face the hurt in her heart.

Sometime late in the day Awatamoo brought her a mint-flavored herbal brew. Surprisingly, it relieved the physical pain.

By the next day Libby managed to drag herself and the water basket to the stream to fill her water pot. They ate well that morning—dry corn bread and boiled salt beef—booty from some unfortunate colonist's home. To Libby and Mary it tasted wonderful. But Libby noticed the Indians grimacing as they ate. They disliked salt, John had told her.

After breakfast she and Mary must shoulder their packs. Libby carried blankets this time—they acted as padding—and found a branch she could use as a walking stick. But she could not keep up. She did not see John anywhere in the group.

Once during the dull misery of the day she caught a glimpse of Ishmael. *Why does he watch me?* she thought. She could not meet his eyes. "Judas!" she whispered.

That night they camped in the open, huddled near the fire beneath leather robes. She was nearly asleep when John and his Indian master stumbled into the clearing. John moved like a sleepwalker, but fury blazed from his eyes. He dragged a robe to a spot near Libby and collapsed. "Killing's too good for them," he said. "I'd like to ship them all to the West Indies for slaves."

In spite of her own anger, John's words set Libby's stomach churning. What had happened to the kind, dependable friend she remembered? She did not like the replacement. *He's as bitter as Ishmael,* she thought, *but with far less reason.*

We're all playing a ridiculous game, she realized. *It's our duty to escape. And their duty to stop us. And none of us remember why.*

They stumbled on the next morning without food. Mary fell several times, but Libby could not help her up. Only the sturdy stick kept Libby erect.

She did not see John again. But several times Ishmael started to approach her, then drew back. She ignored his advances. But when they camped that night he crept up behind her and laid a hand on her shoulder.

"Ow!" Libby winced away from his touch.

"Libby!" Ishmael's voice cracked midword. "I'm sorry. I didn't know you would be there."

Libby wouldn't look at him. "But you meant to hurt John."

"I was wrong, Libby. I thought I wanted to see John hurt. But-but when it happened I knew I was wrong. I'll never do that to anyone again. Can you forgive me?"

Libby thought carefully. "I don't know, Ishmael. I-I want to. Hating makes me sick. But you've managed to turn John into as big a monster as you are." She heard Ishmael stifle a sob. "I'll try, Ike. But I feel so alone."

"I know I don't deserve to be forgiven, but I had to tell you."

"I'm glad, Ishmael," Libby told him. "As God is my helper, I'll try."

Ishmael slipped into the shadows.

Libby slept little that night. The next morning Libby and the others straggled on. Sometimes she forgot that she had ever done anything but pick her way through snow and ice. Then one foot sank into the slush. "It's melting, Mary. Spring will come."

In front of Libby Mary straightened under her pack, and stepped out briskly. A few steps later she sagged again. "What difference will it make?"

Two days later they made temporary camp. No one had eaten anything except broth for three days. Some of the men and boys set snares for rabbits. Several musket-carrying braves drafted Ishmael as carrier and went hunting. Everyone hoped they would bag larger game.

In camp a few little boys tried to fish. Awatamoo thrust yarn and knitting needles at Mary and Libby. By listening and watching carefully they deciphered her orders: Make stockings for little Weetashonks. Both girls enjoyed the task.

Weetashonks watched them eagerly. Finally Mary found two small, but sturdy sticks, notched them, and tried to teach her.

Libby smiled as Weetashonks tried valiantly to cast yarn onto the makeshift needles. A few minutes later the little girl had tangled the yarn hopelessly. She stared at it soberly, then giggled. Libby laughed with her. Hearing them, Awatamoo smiled beneath her paint.

In midafternoon Ishmael's hunting companions returned without him, but they carried the carcass of a settler's pig gone wild. That night they feasted. For the first time since Lancaster Libby's stomach felt full. She refused to wonder about Ishmael. He could take care of himself anywhere.

The moon glowed in the icy clear sky when Libby and Mary made a final trip to the bushes before bed. Just beyond them Libby heard the bushes crackle, then a low moan. Mary let out a frightened squeak, and fled toward the lodge.

Libby leaped after her, then stopped in midstride as someone moaned again. "Who's there?" she called, forming the unfamiliar Algonquian words carefully.

"Ishmael."

Swallowing her fear, Libby turned toward his voice. "Where are you?"

A twig snapped again, guiding Libby.

He lay in a little hollow between two trees, silhouetted vaguely in the firelight that seeped around the hanging mat in the lodge doorway. "What is it, Ishmael?"

He moaned again.

"Don't play games with me," Libby snapped. "I know you too well to believe you're hurt." She moved closer, half expecting him to grab her.

"I think my leg is broken," Ishmael said.

"Surely not." But Libby knelt beside him, trying to see.

"Can you straighten it out?" he asked.

"Which one?" She moved out of reach of his arms.

"The right."

Starting at his ankle she felt along the leg. Halfway between ankle and knee it bent oddly. When she touched it, he snatched at her skirt to muffle a cry of pain.

"You're right, Ike. It's broken. What happened?"

"The stupid pig charged me and knocked me down while we were hunting. When they saw I couldn't walk, they just left me. I crawled back."

"Why here?"

"I had to move or freeze—and-and there was no place else to go."

"Let me get help," Libby said.

"Who's to get?"

"I'll find somebody. Don't worry."

Libby hurried back to the lodge, to find Mary singing a lullaby to Weetashonks while tears dripped slowly down her nose. "I'm back, Mary," Libby called. "It was Ishmael making the noise. He's hurt."

"Good."

"No, Mary. As long as we don't hate back, the Indians can't destroy us. But when we hate we're as bad as they are. Just keep singing to Weetashonks. I'll be back."

"All right."

Quickly Libby made her way to the lodge where John slept, and stepped through the door hangings. "John! We have an emergency!"

"What can I do? They watch us all the time."

"Just listen. Ishmael broke his leg hunting this afternoon. He managed to crawl back to camp. You know how to set it don't you?"

"Not his."

"John!"

"The answer is no, Libby. He's a Judas, and if he's hanged himself it's fine by me."

"Then tell me what to do."

"I will not." John turned to stare at the fire.

Whirling, Libby streaked through the door into the icy evening. She had to do something. But what? If she stayed out much longer, Awatamoo would come looking for her. She did not notice the Indian who followed her until he spoke to her in English. "I can help."

"Why would you?" she asked.

"I'm Printer James—I was a Praying Indian."

"I've heard of you. You sided with Philip."

"I can help you," James repeated. "I cannot forget the teachings of Jesus. Where is your friend?"

They found Ishmael a few yards nearer the camp than when Libby had left him. Libby took his hand. "Hang on, Ike. Printer James is going to straighten your leg if he can."

Ishmael lay silent, his mouth muffled in Libby's skirt, as James worked. But Libby nearly cried out from the pressure of his hand on hers.

"I'll splint it now and get him inside," James promised. "You go back to your mistress before she gets angry."

Awatamoo looked up as Libby slipped inside the lodge for the final time. To Libby's relief Awatamoo showed no sign of anger. In fact, she smiled.

The following morning they ate again, then broke camp. Libby felt the best she had felt in days. Mary managed a cheerful grin, and Weetashonks seemed livelier.

One of the hunters had reclaimed Ishmael. He hopped awkwardly with the help of a stick, his splinted leg held in front of him. As Libby watched, the hunter fastened a heavy pack on Ishmael's back. He took two hopping steps, then fell.

The Indian kicked him as he struggled to regain his feet. On his next try, Ishmael stumbled onto his injured leg and fell. Libby watched as he bit his lips to keep from crying out. Two more hops and he fell again. The hunter aimed his musket.

Libby couldn't breathe. *Oh, God. Don't let them. I'm sorry I was angry.*

The Indian rammed the powder into the musket, then dropped in a ball. Ishmael tried to roll away. But Indians surrounded him.

Then James stepped between the gun and Ishmael. He said something in Algonquian, handed the hunter a wampum necklace, then leaned down to help Ishmael up. James checked the splint carefully, then hoisted the boy to his back.

Sometime during that day James and Ishmael left the rest of the group. A few days later John, too, left.

Days stretched into weeks. Libby watched snow and ice recede. Azaleas and dogwood bloomed along the trails. *It's more than a year since Father and I came to Boston,* Libby realized one day. But London and Lancaster felt a lifetime away. She had no idea what settlements might be near. Even Mary could only guess.

One glorious sunny day Awatamoo beckoned Mary and Libby to follow her. Libby bent down to let Weetashonks ride pick-a-back. Awatamoo flashed her a warm smile, and they set off.

The path led out of the forest into open country. "Look, Libby," Mary said excitedly. "Fenced fields. We must be near a settlement."

They topped a little hill. Below them Libby saw burned-out houses, roads—a few undamaged houses—and people! English people like them!

Awatamoo pointed to the settlement. "Go," she said in English, and gave Mary a gentle shove.

Libby set Weetashonks on the ground, then kissed her impulsively. "Thank you," she said, using the Algonquian words.

Chapter 12

Providence

Taking Mary's hand, Libby walked down the hill. Somewhere below, blue water glistened, and the breeze on her face smelled of salt. In the distance seagulls cried.

"She let us go," Mary said, voicing the words Libby was almost afraid to think.

"I think so," Libby whispered. "Do you know what town this is, Mary?"

"I haven't the slightest idea. Look, Libby. Isn't that a fort?"

As the girls approached, an old man came toward them. "Hello," Libby called, waving. What if he thought they were Indians? *At least we're not greased and painted.*

The man stared at them, then smiled. "You've been with the Indians?" he asked. They nodded.

"I see they released you of their own accord. Welcome to Providence. I am Roger Williams."

The heretic? Rhode Island? Nothing made sense any more. "This is Mary Rowlandson, and I'm Libby Kendall," she said. To her surprise, Libby's eyes blurred. She shook her head vigorously, and swiped a grimy hand across her cheek. "Have you heard of Pastor Joseph Rowlandson in Massachusetts? Can someone get word to The Bay that Mary's safe?"

"We can," the old man said. "And what about your family?"

"There's no one. I'm the Rowlandsons' indentured servant." Suddenly Libby's legs felt like putty. She began to shake. The old man steadied her. "Just a little farther, now. There's not much left of Providence. But we do have food."

Food! She had nearly forgotten her empty stomach. What would it be like to eat a real meal—to feel satisfied again? They had reached a muddy road lined with the charred skeletons of houses. "It's not much farther," the old man encouraged her. "Mary can stay with the Puritan pastor. I'll take you to the Bishops' place. The Indians didn't touch it. Likely you can help Mrs. Bishop until we can get you back."

He turned to Mary. "Your parents are both at The Bay, I believe. I heard that your father ransomed your mother.

"Thank God! But what about Joseph?" Mary asked.

"I don't know. But if I hear anything I'll get word to you," he promised.

They reached the Bishop house just as Libby's legs began to buckle. Mistress Bishop answered the old man's knock. "Good day to you, Master Williams."

Libby's thoughts whirled dizzily. Were they truly safe here? Why was this kindly man banned from Massachusetts? She glanced behind her, half expecting to see Awatamoo.

"These girls just walked out of the forest," Roger Williams told Mrs. Bishop. "This is Mary Rowlandson. Her parents are waiting for her at The Bay as soon as we can get her there. I'm taking her to the Puritan pastor's house. The older girl, Libby Kendall, is their servant. She could be a great help to you while she's here."

"Of course." Mistress Bishop smiled at Libby. "Come in," she said.

Mary clung to her hand. "Don't leave me, Libby," she whispered.

Libby whispered back. "I have to, but it's all right Mary. We're home."

"It's not home without Mother or Father." Mary's voice shook.

"It won't be long now."

Mary straightened her shoulders and put on a smile. "I never thought I'd see the day I'd wish for Joseph. But I do. I hope he's all right."

Libby watched Roger Williams and Mary until they turned a corner. Then she followed Mistress Bishop through the door. Once inside her legs refused to support her. She leaned, shaking, against the wall.

"Come to the settle. Thou must rest and eat. Put thy arm over my shoulder." Mistress Bishop propelled Libby to a seat in front of the fire. Never had a fireplace looked or felt so beautiful!

"Thank you, Ma'am," Libby said.

"Thou must not call me 'you.' We are all equal in the eyes of God. Thou mayest call me Patience."

"You're a Quaker, aren't you?" Libby asked.

"I am."

"We met a Quaker on the ship coming from England," Libby said. "He helped my father when he was sick. Father would have died then without him."

"Thou must eat." Patience filled a wooden bowl with cornmeal porridge laced liberally with molasses, then poured milk into a hollow gourd and setting it on the narrow board, disappeared out the back door.

Libby wanted to eat slowly, savoring each bite. But she could not. She drained the gourd and smiled. Never had anything tasted so good! *I wish I could share some with Weetashonks*, she thought. At least Awatamoo had two less mouths to feed now.

Patience came in carrying a bucket of water which she poured into a large pot over the fireplace.

"When this is hot you can bathe. And I can loan you a change of clothes."

"What can I do to help?"

"Nothing until you have rested and cleaned up."

"Patience," Libby said hesitantly. "There is one thing I'd like while the water heats. Do you have a Bible?"

"Of course. Don't mind the rumors you've heard. Quakers honor the Bible as all Christians do."

Libby turned quickly to Psalm 116. "I love the Lord . . . because he hath inclined his ear unto me, therefore will I call upon Him as long as I live." The first two verses expressed her gratitude perfectly. But what of Ishmael? What of John? She smiled. God had brought her out. She dared hope the same for them. For the first time in months Libby relaxed completely.

Patience woke her when the water steamed. "Your bath water is ready." Together they carried the pot into a bedroom; then Libby scrubbed. Grime covered her body. But at last she penetrated the final layer and her skin felt clean and smooth. As she pulled on the clean fresh undergarments and one of Patience's work dresses, the last worry knot untied itself. Libby stretched herself across the bed and slept soundly.

Patience called her at lunchtime. Libby awakened abruptly and looked around, puzzled. Where was she? Had she lost Mary? Why did Awatamoo let her sleep? She jumped to her feet, half frightened. "Libby," Patience called again. "Come to the noon meal."

"Yes, Ma'am!" Memory returned in a rush. She was safe! She brushed her still damp hair back and settled her cap. In the main room she found a dozen people gathered around Patience's board. Libby could only stare.

"Since our house and provisions were spared, several families eat together here," Patience explained. She introduced everyone, but the names blurred together in Libby's mind.

They ate bean soup and corn bread. This time Libby could eat slowly. She refused seconds. "This is as much as we ate in three days much of the time," she said.

"How long were you with the Indians?" Master Bishop asked.

"Forever, it seemed like!" Libby tried to think. "They took Lancaster February 10. When is it now?"

"The first week in May," Patience told her.

"Then it was about three months," Libby said. "It felt like a year."

"How did you get away?" someone else asked.

"We didn't, exactly. Awatamoo, our owner, brought us to the hill and told us to come in."

"Did they starve you?"

Libby shook her head. "They were starving, too. You'd never believe some of the things we ate. But we stayed alive."

"You were slaves?"

"Yes," Libby said. "But at least once, Awatamoo saved my life. My shoes gave out the first day. She found moccasins for me when I couldn't walk any longer."

"You mean you were well treated?"

Libby thought a long time. "I was lucky except the time John and I tried to escape. They nearly killed me then. They killed little Sarah Rowlandson when they took Lancaster. Once I was sure they would kill Ishmael, a boy from Lancaster." She spread an extra layer of butter on her corn bread. "Have you heard of a Praying Indian who calls himself Printer James?"

"Yes," Master Bishop said. "He is a well-educated man. He helped negotiate Mistress Rowlandson's release."

"I'm not surprised. He saved Ishmael's life, too. I like him."

Libby slept again that afternoon, then ate the evening meal with the others and joined in evening worship.

By the next morning she felt ready to work. "You may stir the porridge," Patience said.

"I'll be glad to." Libby smiled, remembering the first time she had made porridge. How much she had learned! Now she stirred the cornmeal slowly and carefully into the boiling water, and quickly squashed any lumps against the side of the pot. *I'm probably the only girl in New England who is proud of her porridge*, she thought as she and Patience ladled it out. Mary would be proud of me. How strange not to see Mary! Even stranger to know Mary's safety no longer depended on her, Libby thought. *I hope the pastor's wife knows she needs mothering.*

Later that day Libby swept the floor and helped Patience bake bread and prepare fish for the evening meal. The familiar tasks pushed memories of the past weeks out of her mind. Except that today she worked in an unfamiliar house with an unfamiliar mistress, those weeks might not have happened.

The next day was Sunday—First Day, Patience called it. "The names of the days came from pagan gods," she explained to Libby. "We Friends stick to plain speech and call days by their numbers. By the way, meeting is at our house. Wilt thou join us?"

"Yes," Libby said, trying to forget that in Massachusetts Bay Colony she could be fined five pounds for attending. She had no idea what to expect. She knew only that Quakers had no proper clergy. She could not imagine meeting without a minister. They must have some other kind of leader. Libby sat in a corner watching the people come. As they arrived, she sensed an undercurrent of excitement. When all had gathered they simply sat, waiting. Libby couldn't help noticing that not one man removed his hat. At first she thought their leader must be late, but no one came.

Libby had never felt such stillness, such expectancy. Tears streamed down Patience's face, bathing a peaceful smile. *They expect something good to happen*, Libby thought. *But what?*

She sat, enjoying the peacefulness of it all, remembering Isaiah's words in the Bible, "In quietness and confidence shall be your strength." These people possessed both, pressed down and running over, spilling joy on Libby, the outsider. Never again could she doubt God's love.

Once Patience's husband knelt by his chair to pray. Instantly every man in the room removed his hat. When Master Bishop said, "Amen," the hats went back on. Libby glanced at the window. The Bishops had marked the point where the sun's rays fell at midday—a noon mark Patience called it. To her surprise the sun had nearly reached the mark.

Then it happened! A woman Libby had not seen before stood. A woman speaking? Libby tried not to stare.

"The Word became flesh and made His tabernacle among us." The woman's voice flowed in rhythmic cadences. "Yea, He hath visited us, His people. He who is our Daystar from on high. He is here within us, the light to our feet and our lamp lighting the way. The Lord hath given me great openings, and bids me remind thee all, my friends, that thee walk in the light of His love, doing justice, loving mercy and walking humbly before thy God. He is our Alpha and Omega, our end and beginning, and in Him we rejoice."

She paused, then resumed in ordinary tones. "My friends, this week God sent to me a young man who has been held by the Indians. And God opened to me that he walks in the blackness of anger. I spoke to him of Christ, our Light who teaches us all that we need. And he was softened, although he felt not free to join us. Join me in praying that he will look within to the Light that lighteth every man that has come into the world, and find freedom in Him."

Once again every man's hat lay on his chair and everyone knelt. Libby hesitated a moment, then joined them. Who had come out, she wondered. John? Ishmael? Both walked in anger as the woman had said.

As they prayed she realized that she had not heard one definition of sin—not one word of condemnation.

After meeting, the Sabbath or First Day passed much as it had in Lancaster. Libby plied Patience with questions. "I had always heard that you rejected the Bible. But I hear you all quoting it. Why do people say such a thing?"

"You hear a great deal about the Bible being God's Word, don't you?" Patience asked.

Libby nodded.

"Do your pastors speak of Christ, the Living Word?"

"I've not heard them. But I've read it in John."

Patience sighed. "They misunderstand us on that point. We honor and obey the written Word, but we *know* Christ, the living Word. He communicates with each of us—directly. The written Word is not the only way God speaks."

"I see." Libby could find no fault with that explanation. "Why is it that your men refuse to take off their hats to anyone?"

"The Bible tells us to owe no man anything, except to love one another, and that all are equal in God's eyes."

Libby thought a long time, remembering the Apostle Paul's words, "Neither bond, nor free, nor male or female . . . ." Nothing to argue with there. Was she being seduced by the devil? Surely not.

"But why won't you swear in court?" she asked. "I thought swearing showed respect for God."

"Jesus said not to. He said let your 'yes' be 'yes' and your 'no' be 'no.'"

"I've read that lots of times," Libby said thoughtfully. "I guess I never thought about what it means."

Two days later as Libby set food on the board, John came in with one of their regular guests. They stood near the window discussing something earnestly. From the color of his cheeks, Libby guessed that John was arguing.

He didn't notice her until she had filled everyone's trencher and settled herself on the hearth to eat. A moment later John left the other men and came to sit cross-legged beside her. "Libby! How are you faring in this God-forsaken place?"

"Very well, thank you."

"I hope we can find a safe way home, soon." John struck his spoon against the side of the trencher. "This place is a regular hotbed of heresy. Did you know Roger Williams is here?"

"He's the first person we met and one of the kindest people I've ever met," Libby said.

"It's better to stick to true theology than to depend on works."

"How do you know our theology is the whole truth?"

John stared at her. "Why we hear truth preached every Sunday when we are at home."

"How do you know? Has God confirmed what you hear in your own heart?"

John's cheeks flamed, but he controlled his voice. "Libby, what's come over you? Are these Quakers converting you?"

"Absolutely not, John Morris! I can think for myself. Nobody here has said one thing that I hadn't read in my Bible."

"There *is* something different about them," John admitted. "Their words of Christ draw me. But how can I trust myself? I shan't be misled by feelings. How could I face my father or pastor—or anyone if I let them subvert me?" He twisted his hands in his lap. "They can't be right, Libby. It would destroy our entire lives."

"English Puritans and Quakers have both uprooted their lives for what they believe is God's truth," Libby said. John didn't answer. "When did you come in?" Libby asked, finally.

"I got away a week ago. The war's nearly over, Libby. They're about to give up, and the fewer captives they hold then, the better. When did you?"

The woman at Meeting *had* spoken of John! Libby smiled. "Awatamoo brought us here about the same time."

"We could have settled this war long ago if these people had helped," John said.

"They have helped," Libby declared. "Their deputy governor John Easton did everything he could to keep it from starting. And you've surely noticed whose houses weren't burned. They say it's our war, not theirs."

Anger drained from John's face to be replaced by worry. "Don't, Libby. You're being corrupted. Do you know what would happen to you if anyone at The Bay heard you talking like that?"

"Have you been to any Quaker meetings, John?"

"No." For a moment John looked wistful. "And I will not go. If you're wise, you won't either."

"I have, already," Libby said, "and I felt truth there. But don't worry. I'll go back to The Bay and I'll say nothing. I have to work the rest of my time."

Chapter 13

Return

Libby, canst thou finish dinner?" Patience asked. "The Lord has told me that Sarah Cobb needs my company this morning."

"Of course," Libby said, surprised. She studied Patience's face thoughtfully. Six months ago she would not have believed that God told living people anything except through the Bible. But if Patience said God told her to go, Libby believed her.

Libby turned back to the fireplace abruptly, hoping Patience hadn't seen her stare. "God go with thee," she said, stumbling over the unaccustomed words.

Libby stirred the simmering beans, replaced the lid on the pot, and got out trenchers for the usual guests. As she laid trenchers and spoons in place, someone knocked.

She glanced at the noon mark on the window. The sun had not yet reached it. Whoever knocked wanted more than dinner.

Libby opened the door and John burst through. "We're going home, Libby! We'll have an escort into Massachusetts, and militia members will meet us and take us to The Bay."

"When?" Libby demanded.

John smiled. "Tomorrow. If you have anything to pack, pack it. We'll leave at sunup. Home, Libby!

Can you believe it?" John twirled his hat on one finger, then tossed it into the air. "Home, Libby!" he repeated. "Anywhere in Massachusetts with Puritans is home. You can't know how I missed it!"

"No, I can't," Libby said honestly. "I miss people more than places. I hope Mrs. Rowlandson is well."

"I hope I've helped keep you from being homesick, Libby."

Had he? Perhaps, but not in the way he meant. "You've certainly given me plenty of here and now to think about," she told him.

"I'd like to give you more," John said soberly. "I worry about you, Libby."

"For pity's sake, why?"

"You're far too cozy with the Bishops and their Quaker meeting. I'm glad we're leaving before you lose your head—and your soul completely. You know I like you a lot."

Enough of that! Libby thought. Aloud she said, "It's nice of you to worry, but I'm in God's hands; that's safety enough."

John clamped his lips together in a hard line. "I hope you're right." To Libby he sounded unconvinced. "I know Mistress Rowlandson will be pleased at the way you watched over Mary. It was clever of you to make up to Awatamoo's little girl."

"It wasn't clever at all," Libby said. "I did it because—because she was a little girl. I couldn't stand to see her sick. I hope she's getting enough to eat, now!"

"What difference does it make?" John asked. "If we ever win this war, and I think we will, likely she'll be sold into slavery."

"They wouldn't!"

"Yes, they would! It's been done before."

Libby shuddered. "I'll see you in the morning, John." She turned to stir the pot of bean soup over the fire.

The door slammed as John went out. Libby picked up the trenchers, humming to herself. But beneath her excitement she felt a current of uneasiness.

Forget it! she told herself. *You've done nothing wrong and you know it.*

By the time Patience returned to preside over the noon meal, thoughts of home drove everything else from Libby's mind.

"Someone's here to see you, Libby," Patience announced as she came in.

Libby looked up to see Ishmael. His clothing hung in tatters and he leaned on a homemade crutch, but happiness radiated from his smile.

"Have you heard the news, Libby?" he asked. "We're going home."

"Yes. John's here and he stopped to tell me."

For once Ishmael didn't scowl when she said John's name. But for a moment he looked troubled. Then the smile returned, a genuine smile that spoke true joy. "I'm glad," he said. "It's been hard for him."

Libby stared. The Ishmael she knew would never say such a thing.

When Libby began to clear up after the meal she found Ishmael at her elbow. "Can I help?"

Libby stared again, then collected herself. "Surely. Can you fetch a new bucket of water to replace what I'm heating?"

"At your service!" Now that sounded more like Ishmael. He hobbled to the door. She had forgotten his bad leg, Libby thought remorsefully.

"I'm sorry," she told him when he stumped in, dowsing himself in splashes from the half-filled bucket with each step. "I forgot your leg."

"I didn't mind, really. Is this enough?"

"Yes."

Ishmael balanced himself on his crutch across the board from her as she washed the dishes. "Libby, I-I hope you weren't laid up too long after-after I left."

"I was already better when I found you that night. Awatamoo gave me some kind of herbal tea that helped a lot."

"I'm glad." For the second time Ishmael met her eyes directly. *Something's changed him,* she thought. *What's happened?*

"I've done a lot of thinking," Ishmael told her. "And the more I think, the more ashamed I feel. Can you forgive me?"

Libby blushed, remembering her response the last time Ishmael asked. But her anger had fled the night she found him lying hurt in the bushes.

She smiled across the dishpan. "I already did."

"I guess I'm glad John's here," Ishmael continued. "I need to apologize to him again, too. I won't blame him much though, if he ignores me."

"Ike, what's happened to you?"

"It's a long story. I thought at first it began with James—but I guess you started it when we read together. James believed God loved me like you said He did! I had always supposed all God wanted was to catch me sinning so He could punish me. James showed me I was wrong."

"I'm glad you believe it," Libby said. "Did James get into any trouble when he spoke up for you?"

"I'm not sure. Maybe that's why we left the group we were with," Ishmael said. "We went to Meta-comet's—Philip's headquarters. At any rate James kept me safe and made me think. And he saw to it I came here. Let me."

Ishmael took the dish towel and began to wipe the clean dishes. "James said he tried running away from God. But he didn't like it. He's coming out, Libby, as soon as he can. Meantime he's trying to help the captives." Ishmael changed the subject abruptly. "Libby, have you been to Quaker Meeting?"

"Yes."

"What did you think?" Ishmael asked.

"These people talk to God and they hear Him answer. They know they are saved, and they act like Jesus acted in the Gospel stories." Libby stacked the trenchers and set them on a shelf.

"They convinced me," Ishmael said. "Here I'm not charity. I'm not a half-breed. I'm a real person. They-they love me. Nobody ever did that—not much, anyway. And God has revealed Himself to me, too."

"What will you do now?" Libby asked.

"I'm going home." Ishmael said. "But I'll come back to Providence as soon as I can. I've always been a burden to the Kerleys. They won't miss me. But they did feed and clothe me and try to educate me. I want to thank them and apologize for the bad time I gave them."

Unshed tears clogged Libby's throat. "I'm glad for you, Ike. There's truth here, and love. I try not to think of it, because I want to go back to Rowlandsons. But I can see how you've changed. I hope they can, too."

"I hope John can," Ishmael said. "I'm scared to talk to him."

"I hope so, too." Libby hung the last pan back on its peg beside the fireplace.

Ishmael balanced on his crutch turning his hat in his hand. "I'll see you tomorrow, Libby."

"The Lord go with thee." This time Libby didn't stumble over the words.

After prayers that night Libby assembled her bundle—the clothes she had worn in captivity, now neatly mended, and the outfit Patience had given her. "I shall miss thee," Patience said.

"I shall miss thee, too," Libby said. "But I love the Rowlandsons. I'm glad I'll be with them three more years." Libby bound the bundle tightly with a leather thong. "But I'm glad I came to you. I want to be right, Patience, to walk in all the light God has for me. And you've made me think and pray."

"I know, Libby," Patience said. "My prayers will follow thee to The Bay. Thy conscience is tender toward God."

"Isn't it presumptuous to expect God to talk to you?" Libby asked. "I know Pastor Rowlandson would say so."

Patience smiled. "Presumptuous? Perhaps. But He does. He promised in Scripture that He would. Paul told the Christians in Corinth that they had the mind of Christ. His Spirit bears witness with our spirit. He intended us to enjoy life in Him."

"He is the light that lights everyone," Patience continued. "Look within and find His light awaiting thee."

"I'll try," Libby promised, wondering what Rowlandsons would think of such introspection.

Before dawn next morning Libby posted herself by the window waiting for the sun to creep over Naragansett Bay. She could see its first light when she heard voices outside. She looked out to see John striding toward the door with Ishmael limping behind. John reached the door first. In the dim light she saw him scowl at Ishmael. When she stepped outside to join them, she saw Mary run toward her. "Libby!" she jumped up and down with excitement. "Joseph's home, Libby! Master Williams just told me. He came out last week. We'll all be together again—" her voice broke. Libby gathered Mary into the circle of her arm. They both dreaded seeing the family without Sarah.

The main party walked, but Ishmael mounted a pony. "Roger Williams loaned him to me," he told Libby. He twisted his head to see Providence behind them. Libby turned and walked backward beside him. "Goodbye," Ishmael said.

"Goodbye," Libby echoed, wondering when or if she would see Patience again. But John never looked back.

All day Libby and John walked behind Ishmael's pony. Ishmael kept him at a sedate walk. He handled the reins gently, Libby saw. He even spoke gently and patiently to his mount.

That night they stayed at an inn run by Quakers; Indians had burned many Puritan inns. Ishmael fed and groomed the pony himself before he joined them at supper. *A miracle!* Libby thought, remembering Ishmael's cringing puppy.

By morning John regained his smile, but Ishmael grew sober. "Did you talk to John?" Libby asked.

"Yes. But he wouldn't listen. I thought he might hit me, but at least he didn't go that far." Ishmael winced at the memory. "I wouldn't have blamed him much. I had it coming."

"I'm proud of you, Ike."

"I'm getting scared, now," Ishmael admitted. "My foster mother does care about me a little. She'll think I've gone to the devil for sure. As for Mr. Kerley—" he rolled his eyes. "I've told my last lie, so I'm in for it, I guess."

They all rode horseback that day—Libby riding pillion behind John. He talked excitedly about his family, wondering about his mother and stepfather. "I wonder how war has affected his business, Libby."

"Maybe it didn't," Libby said. "Indians can't stop ships from England."

"Yes, but can people afford to buy?"

"I don't know," Libby said, "but they will need to replace what they lost."

They rode silently for a long time. "I'm ready to go back to Harvard next term," John told Libby as they passed through a village. "When I'm finished I'll take a church if there is one. If not, I'll work for my father. I could marry then."

"I couldn't," Libby said quietly.

"I could pay off the indentures."

"I'm not sure that would be right. Rowlandsons are the only family I have, and they've lost everything. They will have work for me to do. I won't think of marriage until I've worked off my indentures."

Like the Rowlandsons, the Kerley family was staying with friends in Boston until it was safe to return home. Ishmael left their group first. Then they reached the Rowlandsons' door. "Mary!" Mistress Rowlandson hugged the little girl tightly, then stepped back to look at her. "You've grown thin!"

"So have you, Mama."

"Did they hurt you, Mary?"

"No, Mama. But we were slaves. And they hurt Libby. I was a slave, too."

Mistress Rowlandson pulled both girls close. "What happened, Libby?"

"John Morris was in our camp for a while. We were planning to escape. They found out and punished us. But our mistress was kind." For a moment Libby thought of Weetashonks. But she could not talk about her. She caught herself watching to see Sarah peek around her mother's skirt.

"Our mistress let us go, Mama," Mary said. "I think she liked us. She had a little girl. Libby and I made her a poppet."

Mrs. Rowlandson smiled at Libby. "Thank you," she said.

"It's good to be home," Libby said. *I'll work my head off while I'm here*, she decided. *This truly is my home.*

That Sunday they all walked to the meeting house. "You sit with us," Mistress Rowlandson said. "We're all displaced here, and we need to be together."

"Thank you."

How good to sing the familiar psalms! Libby had missed singing at the meeting in Providence. Everyone sat, primly glad to be in meeting, but expecting nothing except the long sermon. The sermon dragged into its second hour. Several times Libby saw the tithingman tickle a drowsy-looking woman with his feathers. Once he bonked a sleeping man on the head.

This preacher spent as much time denouncing sins and people as Master Rowlandson used to do.

Chapter 14

A Forced Choice

Mrs. Rowlandson covered her face with her hands. "Libby! Has this heresy affected you, too?"

Did I really say that? I can't hurt her, Libby thought. *But how can I keep quiet? Can't they see God at work in Ishmael?* "I don't know," she said at last. "I don't want to be influenced. But surely you see how different Ishmael is. Can you blame the evil one for that? I love you, and I shall not think of them."

Mr. Rowlandson scowled. "Then they have influenced you! Have you nothing more to say for yourself?"

"As long as I work under your roof I will have nothing to do with them," Libby repeated. Surprised, she heard herself continue. "But last First Day I experienced the presence of God in our midst and He spoke peace and love to my heart. Are we Puritans God's only servants?" Libby heard a shocked gasp from everyone but Ishmael.

"We are," Mr. Rowlandson thundered. "You may retire to the loft until time for the next sermon." Libby obeyed silently.

She spent the next day sewing for Mistress Rowlandson. No one smiled. No one spoke unless giving an order. Even Mary avoided her. After evening prayers Mr. Rowlandson called her aside. "Do you not understand the abominable heresy of these people? They claim to be free from sin. They devalue the Bible."

"Have you spoken to any of them?"

Mr. Rowlandson glared at her. "Of course not!"

"Then, how do you know?" Libby asked.

"Elizabeth! Don't you understand the seriousness of your position? You've seen pillory. And you saw the Cart and Whip Law enforced the day I took you to Lancaster. I would not have that for you."

"Thank you. I love you all. You deserve it. I couldn't—wouldn't do anything to embarrass you. And I do not reject our beliefs. But something in me cries out to know more of God's presence and to rejoice in it. I cannot change that. Is it wrong?"

"When it leads you to the company of heretics, yes. As for embarrassing us, you did that when you spoke up for Ishmael."

Libby didn't answer.

During the days that followed Mr. Rowlandson plied her with anti-Quaker tracts and proof texts to study. Each evening he expected her to summarize and evaluate her reading and to show some sign of repentance. Libby read faithfully and summarized accurately. But she could find nothing to repent of. She was not a Quaker, nor did she plan to join them. Was it wrong to show them respect? In her prayer time she begged God to show her the truth.

It would be easier for me if Quakers were everything Mr. Rowlandson says, she thought. She could not honestly dismiss Quaker teaching. Neither could she accept it.

Ishmael met her near the well on Friday morning. "There's a Quaker meeting here in Boston," he told Libby. "I'm going on First Day. Wilt thou come with me?"

"I'd love to," she said, "but I can't. I promised Mr. Rowlandson I'd do nothing to embarrass them."

Ishmael frowned. "I thought you had more spunk."

"I've no choice," Libby said. "I guess spunk is your department. I try not to think of Quakers at all. Can you really go?"

"Of course I can as long as no one catches me. I've been going where I pleased for more years than they know. I hope I can find someone traveling back to Rhode Island soon."

"So do I. I'm afraid for you here."

Ishmael squared his shoulders and looked into her eyes. "Don't worry, Libby. As God is my helper, I'll follow His Light forever."

Libby grinned at a sudden thought. "You might travel safely alone dressed like an Indian."

"Libby!" Mistress Rowlandson called from the porch. "Come in." Libby ran, splashing water against her skirts at each step. "From now on you must not see Ishmael," Mistress Rowlandson told her. "He seems to be the source of your folly. My husband was right when he tried to discourage your friendship with him. He is beyond redemption, but we still have hope for you."

What kind of redemption makes people fight one another and practice cruelty to those they love? Libby bit her tongue to keep the thought from flowing into words. If that was redemption she wanted no part of it. For the first time she wondered if she could survive the next three years.

Sunday dragged by while Libby wondered about the Boston meeting. Pastor Rowlandson quizzed her on Bible teachings and on her own personal beliefs. "You answer well," he finally told her. "But I know you harbor rebellion and unbelief. If you do not show repentance, I shall have to take you to court."

Libby stared at him, shocked. She had not broken one rule of conduct since her return. Was it a criminal act to defend Ishmael? *Not in Rhode Island*, she thought. Resolutely she shoved all thoughts of Rhode Island, Patience, and Quakers into the back recesses of her mind. *I hate upsetting Rowlandsons,* she thought. *But I can't repent if I can't find anything to repent from.* Nor could she lie. How dare anyone lie about repenting!

John came Tuesday night. "Thank God, we're back home, Libby. Mr. Rowlandson has given me permission to call on you."

"I suppose you're what he calls a good influence," Libby said bitterly. "I'm sorry John. I shouldn't have said that. You've been a good friend—my first friend in the New World."

"I want to be a good influence," John told her soberly. "What happened to you in Rhode Island?"

"Nothing I wouldn't forget if people gave me a chance. I learned it was possible to know God, but that's not heresy. It's what all Puritans want."

John frowned. "But you can't be sure."

"You were sure about Father."

For a moment John seemed puzzled. "That was different."

"How?" Libby asked. "Because he's dead? Jesus said God was the God of the living." She hesitated. "John, the Bible is full of stories of God speaking to people. Why can't it happen today? How else can you explain the change in Ishmael?"

"He's playing up to you—trying to make you like him."

"That's stupid!" Libby told him. "I like him because He's Ishmael, not for the way he acts."

John sat silent, evidently giving up the argument. Finally he spoke. "Libby, if you don't show some sign of repentance you'll end up in court, and you'll never leave unpunished."

"What can they punish me for? I'm not a Quaker. What have I done?" Libby asked.

"You like them and you attended one of their meetings."

"But that was in Rhode Island, not here. And they met in the home where I stayed."

"You didn't have to go," John said. "Don't say I didn't warn you." He stood up. "Libby, won't you reconsider? Please! I-I really care about you." He turned toward the door.

"Reconsider what?"

John stared at her, scowling. Libby met his eyes. If only she could read his thoughts!

John's blue eyes wavered before her gaze, then examined the floor. "I'm not sure, Libby. I'm not sure of anything except that there are some things I mustn't think about." He strode across the room and grabbed her hand. "Think, Libby. You know what it is to be a dissenter."

"I'm not." Libby said. "But if I had to dissent to be right with God, I would. I'm not afraid."

To Libby's surprise John blushed. "I would be afraid, Libby," he whispered. "Maybe I need you for your courage. Try to stay out of trouble—please."

He is afraid, Libby thought. She smiled. "I'm trying, John. I'm glad you understand a little."

"Good night, Libby." John glanced toward the Rowlandsons, then squeezed her hand. She stood watching until the door clicked shut behind him.

The next day Mr. Rowlandson cornered her. "You may not go out, Libby, until you repent. And you are not to talk to Mary. You will do your bidden chores in silence. Then return to your sleeping place. We will not have Mary contaminated."

"I wouldn't!" A sick feeling gripped Libby's stomach. Had she lied to John when she said she wasn't afraid?

In the days that followed no one spoke to her. At meal times she carried her food to the sleeping loft and ate alone. During family prayers Mr. Rowlandson ordered her to perch at the top of the ladder stair.

That Sunday she walked to meeting between the Rowlandsons. As they entered the church hostile stares greeted her from every side. *It couldn't be worse if I really were a heretic*, she thought. She forced a smile and stared straight ahead through tears that refused to fall.

"Have you changed your attitude, Elizabeth?" Mr. Rowlandson asked her on the way home.

"I believe that Jesus atoned for my sins and that He empowers us for living," Libby said.

Mistress Rowlandson pounced on her words. "Are you trying to say you are without sin?"

"Of course not. But not deliberately! I couldn't!"

"Stop thy tongue, Elizabeth! Every word brings you closer to heresy."

Libby said no more. *They love me. They're only doing it for my own good. I should be grateful.* But fear crowded out every other feeling.

That night Libby tossed restlessly on her straw tick. Just as sleepiness overtook her, she felt a tug at her shoulder. Even in the dim light she recognized Mary's shadow.

"Libby!" Mary whispered. "I miss you. Why can't you be good? After Mama I love you more than anybody in the whole world."

Libby forced a whisper past the lump in her throat. "I'm not really being bad, Mary. I just can't make your parents understand what I think." She paused, wondering if she could say what she knew she must. "I miss you, too, dreadfully. But don't come sneaking to talk to me again." Libby brushed away the tears collected on her eyelashes. "Mary, there are three important things you must do. First, love Jesus. Second, love your parents. Third, obey them."

"But it's not fair," Mary sniffled. "Why can't you do what they want? Don't you love me?"

"Yes, I love you. I want to cry every time I walk by you without saying anything. But I can't admit I did something wrong when I don't know what it is. Now go back to bed." Mary turned, still sniffling, and crawled into her own bed.

Libby flopped on her stomach, muffling her tears in the straw tick. For the thousandth time she begged God to show her her sin. "I'd repent, if I only knew I'd done something wrong," she whispered. She lay awake, watching until the night faded, and a faint gray light showed through cracks in the roof.

When Mistress Rowlandson called her, Libby dragged herself erect and stumbled down the ladder. All day she forced herself to work fast. She refused to meet Mary's eyes or even look at her.

When Mr. Rowlandson questioned her that night, Libby countered with a question of her own. "Just what is it I should repent of? Is it that I respect the Quakers I have known? That I recognize God at work in their lives as He is in ours?"

"Precisely that!" Mr. Rowlandson answered. "You must know, Elizabeth, that we all live with our souls in mortal danger. There is no room in a Christian's life for tolerance. We must show no pity, for we are 'brands snatched from the burning.'"

"I understand," Libby said. "But what did Saint Paul mean when he said, 'Who art thou that condemneth another man's servant? To his own master he standeth or falleth'? Wasn't he telling Christians not to judge one another?"

While she watched, Mr. Rowlandson's face turned red, then purple. But he did not shout. "Such an answer is sheer impertinence to your betters, Elizabeth." The words hung ominously in the air. His quiet intensity frightened her more than any shouting could have. "You are dismissed, Elizabeth. Leave my presence immediately."

Libby scuttled up the ladder and collapsed on her straw tick. *Now I know exactly how Ishmael felt*, she thought. *No wonder he was bitter!*

At morning prayers the next day, Mistress Rowlandson's eyes looked red and puffy, as though she had been crying. Guilt stabbed at Libby. Mr. Rowlandson read from the Gospels, declaiming Jesus' descriptions of hell. Libby cringed, knowing he directed his words to her. She saw Mistress Rowlandson gulp back a sob.

After prayers Mistress Rowlandson spoke to her. "Libby, my husband has reported you to the authorities. He has given bond so that you may remain here until your hearing next week." Her voice shook.

"I'm sorry," Libby said without thinking.

"Then why haven't you told him?"

Libby thought carefully. "I'm sorry I made you so miserable. Honestly, I'm no Quaker. I guess my only sin is not hating them. All the time Mary and I were captives, I fought to keep from hating because I believe God condemns it. I will not hate anyone."

"There's logic to what you say," Mistress Rowlandson admitted. "But nothing will move Joseph, now."

For a moment Libby thought the world had stopped, leaving her spinning without it. Fear tasted brassy in her mouth. *Lord, help me. I don't know what to do!*

Libby awoke on court morning with a sick feeling in her stomach, but she forced herself to eat. Who knew when she could get another meal?

Boston's idle souls packed the courtroom, talking and joking, until the magistrate called the court to order. At first Libby could not find a friendly face. Then she saw John sitting on one side of the courtroom. But no Ishmael? Had he taken warning and left? Or had the Kerleys found some way to keep him away? For a moment she imagined him imprisoned, awaiting his own hearing.

"Are you a Quaker?" the magistrate asked her.

"No," she answered firmly.

"Have you contacted any Quakers in Boston?"

"No, Sir."

"Have you any intention to do so?"

"Not during the period of my indentures."

"Will you swear that you are no Quaker?"

Libby's mouth started to form the word "Yes," but the word hung unuttered. "Why did Jesus tell His disciples not to swear?" she asked finally. "Why does the book of James repeat the command?"

"Will you swear on the Bible that you are telling the truth?" the magistrate repeated, and thrust a Bible at her.

Why not? Swearing in court never bothered Father. Why should it matter to me? As her mouth opened, she seemed to hear Jesus' words to His disciples: "Swear not at all."

Chapter 15

Ishmael Intervenes

Libby's hands trembled as she handed the Bible back. "I cannot."

The magistrate banged his gavel. "You have condemned yourself," he shouted. "Yet there may be hope for you. You are hereby sentenced to a day in pillory on the common. It is the hope of this court that this mild punishment will restore you to the path of truth. You will serve the sentence immediately." He banged the gavel again. "Court dismissed."

No more than she had expected! But Libby felt herself sway dizzily. Two officers grabbed her roughly and hustled her out of the room. At first she scrambled to keep up with them. Then she lost her footing and they dragged her like a sack of meal. *Why did I say that?* she asked herself. *Am I a Quaker without knowing it myself?* She scrambled to regain her footing.

In the cool outside air, Libby felt better. *I lied to Mistress Rowlandson,* she thought. *I do hate them all! It's easier that way.*

When they reached the commons the men shoved her head roughly into its hole, letting her bonnet hang down her back.

They ripped off her shawl, tossed it to the ground, and secured her arms tightly.   There she must stand, helpless, until someone released her.

"See the pretty miss with no bonnet!" someone jeered.

"She's a proper godless wench."

For a moment Libby thought she might faint.

"No she's a proper Quaker," someone else called. "She's gray all over."

"Here, miss, catch!" Someone heaved a half-rotten apple toward her. It struck hard against her unprotected face, splattering in all directions. The smell made her retch. Her tormenters only laughed. "It will be worse than this in hell," someone else shouted. Mr. Rowlandson made his way through the crowd. "You have disgraced us, Elizabeth. We shall not trust you again."

For the first time tears stung Libby's eyes. Mr. Rowlandson, himself, had told her to seek God. And she had. Anger filmed her vision with a red haze. Libby caught it just in time. *I can't be angry,* Libby thought. *I got here because I refused to hate Quakers. If I start hating now, it's all wasted. He means well. He really thinks I'm lost. Jesus, help me!*

A rock grazed one cheek. Blood trickled down, tickling her. She shifted her feet, trying vainly to find a more comfortable position. *Maybe I am a Quaker, but if he hadn't taken me to court I wouldn't have known it myself.*

The crowd drifted away. *They executed Mary Dyer,* Libby thought. *And whipped other women out of town. Those women knew what they believed. Do I believe as they did? Oh, Lord, set my feet in the right path.*

Clouds floated across the sun, then blanketed it. Libby shivered. By afternoon rain fell steadily, saturating every layer of clothing she wore. In spite of the rain, a few passersby heaved stones and rotten eggs in her direction. By then, Libby was too cold to care, except when they struck.

Her nose itched. One cheek throbbed where the stone had struck it. Her legs ached, but she dared not fidget for fear of losing her footing in her muddy standing place.

Then she saw a lone woman crossing the deserted common. As the young woman came closer, she stopped to stare, then hurried to her side. "It's me, Betsy Talmadge, remember? I've served my indentures, now."

"Y-yes," Libby shivered.

"What did you do?"

"Th-they think I'm a Quaker because I won't swear."

Betsy retrieved Libby's sodden shawl and tried vainly to secure it around Libby's shoulders. "Are you?"

"I may be someday," Libby said. "They know how to love, not hate."

"That I'd have to see!" Betsy hooted. "Can I do anything to help you?"

"No—yes. Find Ishmael Brown. He's with the Kerley family—at least I hope so. They're refugees from Lancaster. Tell Ishmael to start for Providence NOW! He *is* a Quaker and he's not safe here."

"I'll find him for you. I promise." Betsy exchanged her shawl for Libby's sodden one and strode on her way across the common.

A brisk breeze off the bay pushed the rain inland, leaving Libby colder than ever. Sometime in midafternoon she saw John at the edge of the common. *Afraid*, Libby thought, feeling almost sorry for him.

He lingered until the open field was deserted, then slunk toward her. "Libby, I'm truly sorry. If you're willing to swear you're not a Quaker, I can get the constable to release you. You are ready to give up heresy aren't you?"

"I'm not a heretic. But I can't swear."

"I believe you, Libby, but you're being foolish about swearing. Look, my stepfather promised to loan me money to pay off your indentures. We could even get married."

"Did you ever forgive Ishmael?"

"What does that matter?"

"I'll stay here before I'll disobey God's teaching. And I could never marry anyone who cannot forgive."

John flushed. "Have it your way," he said angrily. "But you'll go to prison. When you're through with your foolishness, remember I'm waiting."

Libby smiled at him. "I am through with foolishness, John. From now on I follow peace with the Quakers."

"Libby!" She watched him turn and plod across the common. *You just lost your first friend in the New World*, she told herself. But she had no choice. Warm tears trickled over the goose bumps on her cheeks. In spite of her own misery, Libby felt sorry for John.

The wind flapped her skirts around her, and she could feel goose bumps spread over her whole body. But suddenly warmth and love filled her with happiness. She had decided. Now she understood Patience's quiet joy. *Jesus is my light, and I know He's in me!* For the first time in her life she understood why the apostles counted it a privilege to suffer for Jesus.

A troop of little boys galloped across the commons on their way home from school. They stopped, to lob stones at her with alarming accuracy. Remembering Stephen's prayer in the book of Acts, Libby smiled at them until a rock split her lip, chipping a tooth.

They ran away at the sound of an adult shout. Libby recognized John's voice. Tears filled her eyes again. He hadn't deserted her.

At last the sun sank low over the hills behind Libby, and the breeze dropped. Dinner hour approached, and pedestrians deserted the common. She began to hope for release. A pony plodded across the common, straight toward her. Then

Ishmael looked down at her soberly. "They sent me on an errand this morning. I didn't know until your friend Betsy found me."

"I told you to leave while you could," Libby said. "You're in enough trouble without being seen with me."

"I'm going. And so are you!"

"I can't!"

"Do you think you're going home tonight? You're not! You'll be in jail—with nobody allowed to visit or bring food—maybe even chained to a log. That's why I came. I won't stand for it, Libby. I can't."

Ishmael slipped from the horse and limped behind her to the catches. He fumbled with them for what seemed a long time. Finally he pulled out his knife and cut the leather thongs that served as hinges for the manacles. Libby collapsed on the ground.

"Get up, Libby! Someone will see us, then it's all over." Libby wobbled to her feet and let Ishmael propel her to the pony.

"You'll have to ride astride," he apologized, boosting her up. "I couldn't get a pillion. This pony can't carry double for too long, but at least I can get us away from town."

Libby didn't reply. Her lip hurt too much. Ahead of them a figure stepped around a tree to stare. John! She saw him cup his hand to his mouth, saw him breathe deeply, saw his adam's apple bob. But he made no sound.

Libby clutched Ishmael's waist tightly as the pony began to trot. "I-I have to pay—" she tried to say between bumps.

Ishmael kicked the pony into a canter. "I know. But first we have to get out of here in one piece."

When at last they reached open country, Ishmael left the main track for an Indian trail, and slowed the pony to a walk. "Let me walk," Libby said. "I can keep up."

"I guess you'll have to. We'll camp in a few minutes. I know a place where no white man will ever find us."

Libby nodded. She felt frozen, separated from everything that had happened. Only the new warmth in her heart seemed real. "Lord, if I have to go, show me how to pay my indentures," she prayed.

When they camped that night Ishmael handed her an almost new Bible. Libby shook her head, pointing to her lip. "Then I'll read." Ishmael opened the Bible to Isaiah. "The people that sat in darkness have seen a great light . . .," he began confidently.

Gradually the world around her became real to Libby again. When he finished, and they had prayed, Ishmael turned to Libby. "Thanks for believing I could learn," he said. "If you could teach me, I reckon you could teach anybody."

So there was a way to pay her debt! She could teach. Mistress Rowlandson had told her the same thing, Libby remembered. Forgetting her lip, Libby smiled, then yelped at the sudden stab of pain.

"You've done just as much for me, Ike," she said softly. "Everything that hurt you made me ask questions. You made me see how important it is for God's people to show love and patience. You made me want Christ the Light in my life."

"Just as you did it for me, Libby." Ishmael paused, then spoke almost timidly. "He brought us together. Do you suppose He meant us to stay together always?"

"I'm too tired tonight to be sure of anything," Libby said, "except that you just told me how to pay my debt. But I hope so, Ike. I can't think of anything I'd like better."